Torn From Normal

By

Martin Bartloff

TORN FROM NORMAL
A Snowflake Book

First paperback printing 2009
Revised 2011

Martin Bartloff
Hampton, Virginia
www.martinbartloff.com

13-digit ISBN: 978-0-615-31072-5
10-digit ISBN: 0615310729
eBook ISBN: 978-0-615-31324-5

PRINTED IN THE UNITED STATES OF AMERICA
10 9 8 7 6 5 4 3 2

For my Parents

Maria Bartloff 1928—2003
Ernst Bartloff 1930—2007

–You will never be forgotten.

For a seemingly, endless amount of professional help, support and devotion, I owe J.R. Turner a book full of gratitude and acknowledgements, but then I'm not even sure words can deliver the acknowledgement she deserves.

I am more than honored to have you work with me from just a ick away. Weeks, months, even years, you have stood firmly by my side and helped me bring Andy to life.

For that I will forever be in your dept.

Thank you! J.R. Turner

For Inspiration and support:

My son Dean, Ryan K, Logan Elliott, Karen Syed, Ophelia Julien, Seth S, the Echelon Press Quake Team.

For all your inspiration and contributions, many thanks to all of you.

PROLOGUE

7:46 a.m., April 3rd

Wind gusted through the half-open window and blew Danny's homework all over the room. Navy cotton curtains floated over his desk like the dark sails of a ghost ship. He tugged the blanket over his face, hiding from the day. Warm breath heated the space between the pillow and blanket, dampening his face. A Coldplay song crept into his head and drew him back into the dream.

Half asleep, he sensed Andy speaking to him; face wet, twisted...glaring. Danny couldn't hear and traveled nearer, desperate to understand. The closer he got, the further away and more silent Andy became. The dark place closed in, shimmering onyx walls pulsing as they squeezed and separated them. He gasped.

The rumble of a dump truck up the block stole the dream away. Sweating, catching his breath, he waited for his brain to understand.

Tuesday.

Did he put the trash out? He tossed the blanket aside and bounded blearily to the window. Rubbing sleep from his eyes, he squinted at the end of the driveway. The cans were there, where he'd set them the night before. He slumped and turned to the bed, the blankets twisted. He gave up on sleep and fled downstairs.

The automated coffee maker burped and gurgled, dripping black liquid and filling the house with the scent of morning. Normally, his dad would be the first one up, zombie-walking to his caffeine, but Danny beat him today. He turned on the television, settling on the couch and switching to MTV. Bright sunlight painted window reflections onto the plasma screen, blocking much of a reality show rerun.

Annoyed, he flipped off the tube. Footsteps overhead; his father was awake. He really didn't want to explain why he was up so early. There had been enough of that lately, that concerned, 'how are you holding up' sort of thing. He returned to his room and tossed on a tank and shorts. Another hot day. Muggy from the coming storm. Like the day it all started.

He gathered his papers from the floor and returned them to the desk. A crow tortured him with a caw loud and brash enough to set his teeth on edge. Though night had been cool enough to keep the window open, he happily closed it now. The big black feathered bird sat on the eaves of the house next door, its dark head cocked as it studied him, judged him as a human gone wrong, mutated into something less.

That Coldplay song returned. Andy's pain and anger returned.

Danny flopped onto the bed and stared at the ceiling. He saw Andy as he searched his house for someone, anyone. He heard him call out, his voice echoed through the single family home. Why wouldn't they answer his desperate shout? Upset, very upset, he threw a chair out of his way. With a curse, he swept the sideboard in the hall clean. The porcelain vase shattered into a thousand pieces on the hardwood floor. He raced upstairs, to his bedroom, breathing hard. His gaze fell instantly on the picture on the nightstand.

He lunged for the frame, ripped the photograph free, and brushed the image with one trembling finger. He wept and wiped the tears with his sleeve. He folded the picture into his back pocket and ran down the stairs. The images wavered, splintered.

Tears blurred Danny's vision. *I should have been a better friend.*

All his stuff in his room, all of it just stuff. The pipes in the walls came alive with the sound of rushing water as his dad got in the shower. Even that noise didn't kill the silence they'd wandered under all fall and winter. Months of thinking and thinking, imagining and re-imagining.

His computer was on and opened to a fresh document. The blinking cursor called him, demanding Andy's story be told.

PART I

Nothing Makes Sense...

CHAPTER 1

Running Away

Andy bit into the roast beef sandwich. The dry bread and leathery meat turned to grains of sand in his mouth. He washed the bite down with water as he read the gazillionth letter he had written. Dumb, he thought and crumpled the paper. He tossed it and his unfinished sandwich into the trashcan.

Too angry to sleep, he debated all night whether or not he should leave a note. What would be the point? Would she even notice he was gone?

Yeah, but only when she got hungry.

He tapped the eraser end of the pencil against his chin as he stared out the one window in his room. It faced a brick wall. Barely enough room for a bed and his desk, the walls painted a sickly gray; he might as well have been in prison. Only he didn't have to spend thirty years tunneling through concrete with a spoon. He planned on walking out the front door.

More than he cared if his aunt knew he was gone, he wanted her to know why he had taken off. Maybe if he had more guts like Jason or knew how to talk the way Danny did, it wouldn't be so hard. But he *was* him and that sucked. Of course with or without a note, she'd probably call the cops on him. After all, if he wasn't there, the government wouldn't give her a check.

Andy smiled darkly at the thought of writing a suicide note. What would she think? Maybe if he wrote he jumped off one of the towers on the Hanover Street Bridge they might not even bother to look for his body. He could just imagine how she'd complain and whine about how bad a kid he was.

He shuddered; happy he would be gone when she discovered he'd left. She would act all sick and helpless then give everyone attitude. All she did was watch TV all day, her fat mutt in her lap as she ate. Jeez, she even had him bring the dog snacks like some stupid servant.

For a dog!

Waiting on them hand and foot was humiliation enough, yet she twisted the screws tighter by saying all sorts of cruel things to him. Things he wanted to hit her for sometimes. Not that he ever would, but man, she made it hard.

Always putting him down, treating him as if he was stupid. She argued over nothing. If he even mentioned how great it had been at Marvin's, she flipped her lid and called him names—most of them starting with, "You ungrateful…"

How could he be grateful about being stuck in a prison cell sized room with no life of his own? He wasn't allowed to call anyone. At first Andy thought she just didn't want to pay for an international phone call to Germany. But when he started dialing his friend Jason's number, she went berserk, snatched the phone away, and made up a story about friends that didn't exist not being able to call her if he tied up the line.

"Besides," she had said, *"What if they get hurt and need*

me? Most of my friends are old, you know. They don't have teenagers running all over the place like I do."

Like Aunt Lily would dash out that door to rescue anyone. Lily to the rescue.

Not!

She wouldn't even let any of his friends call him and he wasn't allowed to answer the phone. He remembered pointing out that it wouldn't cost her any money and that Marvin and Danny would worry about him. Her reply?

"That stupid man. What does he want with another juvenile delinquent to mess up his life? He's not right in the head. Boys need discipline or they end up like your dad. Dying and leaving his family like that. Should have taken better care of himself. Now look at the mess we're in with you living here."

He hated her. She didn't even know Marvin and Danny. They were more his family than she would ever be. She should know the same kind of pain she caused, but he couldn't bring himself to be cruel like that. Not when he knew how much it hurt. He guessed early on how miserable and lonely she was and so held his anger in, let it boil inside, afraid of what might happen every day. He never really understood that whole thing about how misery loved company until now. Only he showed up at her door thinking life couldn't get any worse.

Boy, he was totally wrong. The only time she let him out of the apartment was to walk the dog or buy more food.

Okay, so he couldn't even think about what happened earlier that summer without wanting to puke, but this was like twisting the knife deeper into his gut, living with Aunt

13

Lily. She brought out the worst in him, forcing him into the bottomless pit of her foulness.

Ten days of madness was all Andy could take. This was not how he wanted to live his life—useless, worthless. At seventeen he wanted to be around people who liked him the way he was. Like Marvin and Danny. Any longer under the same roof with her, he would be ready for a shrink.

The notebook lay open, a lined page waiting for his thoughts. How could he tell her, in a way that was fair, how much she sucked? He couldn't, he decided, and chose to just be honest.

Aunt Lily,

Every night I try to figure out what I'm doing wrong so you won't be so mean to me. Just because you didn't like my dad doesn't mean you should get so angry with me. I tried to be nice to you, but that wasn't good enough. You hated me anyway and now I hate you.

He groaned and wadded up the note. Forget it, he thought, I'm not even gonna bother.

The surrounding darkness crept in from the corners, from the blackness beyond his window, and he felt lonelier than ever. Only the light he stared at every night kept him company in the cold room. He often lay in bed, longing to dream of recreated memories so he might at least find some peace in his sleep. The television's flickering, moving light often hurt his eyes from staring too long.

He needed to be as far away from Baltimore as he could

get by the time she woke up. If she didn't notice he wasn't there until she ran out of food, he'd have a decent head start when she called the cops on him.

Andy stood and shoved clothes in the half-full backpack open on his bed. He shook his head. No one listened when he told them this wouldn't work. She didn't want him there anymore than he wanted to be there. In the bathroom, he opened the cabinet door to retrieve his toothbrush. What would it be like in a month, in two months if he stayed? She *wanted* trouble. Then she could take one of her pills and blame it on him. With the money she got for him, she had already bought more.

Andy closed the cabinet door and caught his reflection in the mirror. He could hardly stand to meet his own eyes. The pain there reminded him of all that had happened. Did even God hate him?

Am I really that bad of a kid?

Aunt Lily thought so, but why? This wasn't the face of a psycho, he thought. Dark brown hair, hazel eyes, and some freckles. No way.

He turned off the lights, zipped the last of his belongings inside his backpack, and went to the door. Ear against the wood, he listened. Just the soft sound of the television playing. With care, he turned the knob, afraid to alert the porky little mutt. He snuck quietly toward the apartment door.

Head rolled back against the couch, mouth wide open, the thick white jowls spread beneath her ears pushed up the lobes. The oily grey in her hair shimmered and as he came closer, he noticed for the umpteenth time, that extra long

15

nose hair wagging back and forth in the air. The mutt opened one eye beneath a bushy gray brow. His belly splayed beneath his stubby legs, he was either too lazy or too tired to bark and wake his mistress.

Andy's knees shook as he stepped with care to the front door. The skin between his shoulder blades prickled as he imagined the lights coming on, his aunt throwing herself against the door—as movable as a mountain.

Surprise! She'd grin, baring gums turning green where they met her dentures.

Andy unlocked the door. He checked to make sure the sound hadn't awakened her, and noticed the prescription bottle on the table between them. He stared for a moment, the thought of what he meant to do never fully forming even as he watched himself take the bottle. Make her walk to the store and get her own refill. As soon as his fingers wrapped around the slender, orange cylinder, the mutt grumbled and lifted his head, baring his teeth.

He held still, skin hot with anticipation.

The mutt laid his head back down, still staring at him, but Aunt Lily slept on. Moving quietly, he opened the front door, stepped through, and silently pulled it tight behind him. Only then did he take the moment needed to hide the pills deep in the bottom of a sock before walking down the path and into the night.

CHAPTER 2

Freedom

People, families lived behind each door of the apartment complex, but an eerie silence added a chill to the air. They slept while Andy walked. What kind of people could sleep like that? They must have real families, real lives. The concrete halls of the building bounced his footfalls back, making it sound like someone followed. He stopped, and the echo stopped. A dog yapped, sounding very much like the one on Aunt Lily's lap. Afraid to draw attention, he waited until he'd gotten down the stairs and out the main entrance before he began to run.

Chin tucked down, he ran hard and fast for a good ten minutes without looking back. Night dew flavored air tasted sweet, clean in his mouth. The sidewalks and asphalt sparkled beneath the corner streetlights as if powdered with diamond dust. Light to dark, light to dark, each phase of the getaway offered the fear of being spotted by the police, or mugged in the shadows. Yet even with the danger, a weight lifted from his shoulders.

I'm free!

He grinned and slowed to a purposeful walk. In Virginia Beach he'd been taught a good lesson about walking alone at night. *Show no fear*. He'd learned that one the hard way. Another rule the streets had taught him; have a plan. He hadn't quite figured out that part yet. His plans had only gone as far as getting out of the house. A straight line to anywhere though wasn't a good idea, just in case she did wake and call the police. He turned one corner, than another, in hopes they wouldn't be able to track him.

The further he got from the apartments, the skittish he became. Every small noise goosed his heartbeat. His anxiety grew worse as sad attempts to keep patches of green lawn turned to concrete. Chunks of missing sidewalk became weed beds in front of old boarded up brick buildings.

A fence ran the length of a lot filled with all kinds of cars, tractors, trucks that could have been organized by a blind man. He ran his fingers along the chain link, the pitter-patter hardly a whisper. A big dog charged, barking loud enough to attract the whole world's attention. Andy's heart leapt into his throat as he snatched his hand from the fence and nearly stumbled off the curb.

Inside the house, someone yelled, "Max! Shut up that racket and get back in here!"

Max grunted, whined then hung his head and trotted away.

Andy sighed in relief. He never wanted a dog. He'd rather have a cobra or a skunk. Dog's might be man's best friend, but they sure didn't like him.

Aunt Lily didn't help either. Her favorite game was to sic the bushy-browed mutt on him. For no reason at all she'd goad the dog on by yelling, *"Get 'em boy. Get 'em."*

When he asked why, she said, *"'Cause he's my dog and you ain't gonna be here long. I don't want him to get all attached to you, then go into one of his moods when you leave. I have to wrap his sedatives in cheese!"*

Still, every time she gave Fido a treat for going ballistic on him, he wanted to grab the ever-present bag of chips off the table, hold it high, and make her dance before she could cram them into her wide mouth.

Aunt Lily was so different from Marvin and Danny. When Danny complained about anything, Marvin would grin and sounding like John Wayne, he'd say, *"You wanna hug dere, pardner?"*

Sometimes they would embrace for a brief moment, slapping each other on the back as Andy watched, wishing he was Danny so Marvin could be his dad and he wouldn't be all alone, always the outsider. When they came back, he would just walk up to Marvin and hug him instead of waiting.

Well, maybe if he isn't too mad.

The night air filled him, pumped him up. No one mugged him; no police cars screeched to a stop and hauled him back to the apartment. Even peaceful, he thought, comparing the pre-dawn to Aunt Lily's apartment. Down dark alleys and behind bars, all sorts of bad things happened and yet no one bothered him. A greater being watched over him, finally taking notice.

All the misfortune of the last five years wouldn't hold him back. His dad's heart attack, how his death took away Andy's one chance to go over the road with him, that began the hell that had been his life for so long. No kid should lose a mom or dad, ever.

The sky lightened and an even younger boy rode his bike across the street, a plastic bag hanging from one handlebar. He didn't meet the kid's eyes, looking away as they passed. Strangers always made him uncomfortable. He hated all that awkward small talk where each person tried to figure out if the other was a real tool or cool enough to hang with. The bag swung and *thunked* as the boy pedaled away and he breathed easier.

A true plan took shape in his mind and he smiled. He walked straighter, expanding like a wet sponge after being confined in the stale apartment for so long. At the corner of Bayard and Russell, the road opened wide and he headed south toward the Shell station he was often sent to for Slim Jims and chocolate.

Aunt Lily pointed out once how he could walk to the Greyhound station from there and wouldn't need to even take a taxi, like he had from the train station.

Newport News, Virginia.

His happiest memories were there...until last summer. But he wouldn't think about that now. The last of his money, earned from doing odd jobs for Marvin when he lived with him, would cover a bus ticket. Inside the Shell, he found an old man with white hair, wrinkled black skin, and yellowed eyes.

"No backpacks in here."

"Sorry," Andy said, "I just need directions. Could you point me toward the Greyhound station, please?"

Gnarled fingers rubbed the nubby scrub on his chin then he nodded. "All right. It's that way." He pointed. "Go down to Haines and take a left. Can't miss it. But a kid like you shouldn't be out here alone."

"I'm not," Andy said. "I'm meeting my dad. He's coming

in from Virginia and I just got turned around."

"Okay then." He waved at him. "Just be careful out there."

Andy thanked him and left, hands tucked deep in his pockets. Lying to the old man didn't make him feel all that bad, but lying about his father actually being alive hurt. He wished he could reach Danny and Marvin. Could he even call Europe from a pay phone? Maybe if they knew what was going on, they'd come back early. They left the day after he went to live with his aunt. Ten days was a long enough vacation, right?

The plan flickered and died. Marvin probably wouldn't care so much about coming to help him or leaving Germany early. He would be mad Andy ran away and far worse, he would be disappointed. He'd make him go back to Aunt Lily's and no way was that going to happen. Even Danny wouldn't be able to convince his dad to let Andy stay alone at their house until they got home—and forget about them saying it was okay for him to wing it on the streets. How long did it take to get back from Frankfurt anyway?

Ahead he spotted the station. The only brightly lit area in four blocks. He cut across the filthy parking lot of a nearly abandoned building. Only recent garbage and yellowed curtains in one window indicated people lived there. A car rolled past and the headlights blinded him briefly. The rusty motor ground loud in the after midnight hours. His stomach knotted, worried the car might return, the drivers make him disappear into the heaped trash by the building just for a backpack full of clothes and a toothbrush.

He watched for the car, turning back every few seconds,

until he reached the first part of the station lit by fluorescent lights. Freedom, he realized, was a lot trickier than he remembered, though he didn't remember much about the first time. Funny how he had almost robbed the only real sort-of dad he'd had in years. And Danny was like a brother, even if he almost always took his dad's side.

What if they'd only been pretending? What if Aunt Lily was right and he really was nothing but a burden to them? His friend Jason's family would never let him stay there secretly. Where else could he go? Who else did he know?

No one, really.

He was *not* going back to Lily's apartment.

Not ever!

He'd find a secret place where his aunt, the cops, no one could find him. Marvin promised he could come back if things didn't work out in Baltimore, he had said so the day he put Andy on the train. He only had to wait out the four days until they got back from Europe and everything would be all right. Everything would be fine.

It's gonna be all good, he thought. He could get away with this, hide for four days without getting caught, even if Aunt Lily used the government money to hire one of those P.I. guys, or maybe sent a SWAT team out to find him.

Yeah, that's not gonna happen.

She would get someone else to call, too lazy to do it herself.

Andy turned on to Charles Street, just a block to go. Excited, he jogged the rest of the way. Inside the station, the scent of diesel, grime and body odor lingered in the building. He didn't mind it so much because it smelled like leaving, like an adventure. Only now he was on his own.

He consulted a tattered listing of arrival and departure times affixed to the wall. Unfortunately, he had an hour before the next bus arrived. Exhausted from the walk and deflated anticipation, he sat down on a bench. A soft candy bar served as breakfast. The warm, gooey chocolate filled his mouth, spread on this tongue and he closed his eyes.

He imagined Aunt Lily waking up, screaming for him, getting angrier the longer he didn't answer. When she found him gone, she wouldn't just call the police. No, she'd sic the mutt and the military on him too. Did that mean he was a criminal?

A fugitive?

What if he ended up on *America's Most Wanted*? Jason would totally freak, he'd toss back his dirty blond hair from his pale face and his blue eyes would bug out, for sure. Danny might throw a *Run, Andy, Run!* party—probably not when his dad was home though.

The Marines could come. The Army could come. He knew this was the right thing to do. Waiting at the bus station for an hour was a whole lot better than being in the same apartment with his aunt another day.

CHAPTER 3

Baltimore Dreaming

Though tired from lack of sleep, Andy couldn't get comfortable on the bench. He couldn't remember a night where he didn't have a bed to sleep in—except for camping, but that really didn't count. His lids grew heavy and he yawned so wide, his jaw popped and he closed his eyes.

He dreamed he was already on the bus, going down an interstate somewhere in Virginia and close to home. The sun was bright, the skies clear. Cars honked. Marvin drove his blue convertible beside the bus, dark eyes glancing between the road and Andy. Danny sat in the passenger seat, baseball cap backward, brown hair sticking through the adjustment strap, looking like a younger version of his dad.

All their friends surrounded the bus, driving their souped-up rice burners they decorated with streamers and celebratory soap-paint. Brad's semi-silver Jetta with three aluminum wheels and one donut, growled loudly behind Marvin. Ryan followed in a primer-white Honda two-door coupe with angel-eye headlights and a black hood. Others joined them, each car lowered, muffler over-sized, displaying a mish-mash of spray-painted body parts.

They had come to surprise Andy and welcome him back. Danny scribbled large words on torn cardboard and held up the sign.

Welcome Home, Andy!

Squeaking brakes tore Andy out of the wonderful dream and back into reality. The bus doors thumped wide with a hiss of air. The driver shouted through the open doors as if addressing a waiting crowd of deaf people.

"Baltimore main station, one stop on York Street," the driver called. "Tickets, cash only please."

Andy got up, slung his backpack over his shoulder, and stepped on the bus. From his washed out pair of jeans, he pulled an even more washed out and wrinkled twenty-dollar bill, unfolded it and handed the driver the worn currency. A machine printed the ticket, change clattered into a metal bowl. He made sure to grab every coin, worried the little he had saved working for Marvin would be enough.

"We're earlier than scheduled. We'll leave in just a few minutes. You traveling by yourself?" the driver asked.

Andy nodded.

The driver's brows rose, but he said, "Have a seat please."

Andy sat down third row back behind the driver, unwilling to talk more. Too risky, he could suspect Andy was underage and running away.

Cold, worn and filthy, the bus was not welcoming. Large windows danced to the sound of the engine, panels vibrating. Heart racing, Andy stared at the open front doors. He could still get up, get off, and go back.

Don't lose it.

What would it be like to return to the apartment and face his Aunt? To keep his mind off his doubts, he explored the bus. A chewed up piece of gum was stuck to the cushion of the seat in front of him, a newspaper from the day before lay on a seat to his right.

Don't they ever clean these buses? Gross.

The driver spoke gibberish to headquarters over his radio. The loud engine drowned most of it out even if he could understand. An approaching bus's headlights reflected off the rearview mirror. He squinted and folded his arms together for warmth and to still his trembling hands.

Calm down. Out there he hadn't been half as freaked. He leaned back in the seat and let out a deep breath, expecting to see it plume. Not quite that cold, though. When they got moving, which he prayed was soon, it would warm up. He hoped.

Any minute now, as the sun shone on every pothole and busted window, Aunt Lily would stretch, dazed and yawning. Her shrill voice would rattle the rafters when she hollered. She would sit up, her toes fishing for the hideous felt slippers. Wearing her faded nightgown, she would shuffle like a ghost toward the kitchen, the mutt at her feet eager for the drama, its mangy head stuck high in the air.

Andy, she'd yell, *get up and walk, Fido.* She wouldn't wait for an answer, just storm in, see his bed was empty and all hell was about break loose.

Keep breathing!

The driver of the other bus boarded. Andy rolled his eyes. Now they would stand around jawin' all day. They talked about work then their families and football. Minutes passed as Andy contemplated how he could get them to move faster.

He could tell them he was on his way to see his sickly

26

grandmother. Or better yet, a sick little sister. A little sister who needed his kidney for a transplant or she would die. Thankfully, before he worked up the courage to test the tale out on them, the other driver got off. Relieved, he watched the man walk back to his own bus.

About time.

As passengers trickled aboard, he gazed out the window, expecting Aunt Lily to round the corner at a flesh-bouncing pace, a barking, straining Fido in the lead as a tracking dog.

The hydraulic doors flapped closed, the rubber gaskets clapping together. The lights went off and the driver put the bus in gear. The vibrations ran up the bones of his spine, settling at the base of his head and jaw. Another hiss came from the air brakes then the bus started moving, wobbling back and forth as it gained momentum.

Too late to stop him now, he thought, unless she threw herself in front of the bus. But then he wouldn't have to go home with her because she'd be dead or in the hospital.

They made a wide u-turn around the empty wooden bench where he had napped. Goodbye bench, he thought. See ya, wouldn't wanna be ya.

No turning back.

He had done it all on his own. Tears worked their way to his eyes. He should have been proud of being brave enough to get this far, but he wasn't at all. Defeated, that's what he felt. Like he couldn't hack it and had failed some monumental test.

He swallowed hard, working to keep his self-control. The youngest on the bus, if he got all weepy now, someone might worry enough to remember him if the cops asked them questions later—especially the driver who already made it clear he didn't like Andy on his bus. He kept his face toward the window, staring down every side street, watching every intersection for any sign his aunt or the police wanted to stop and search the bus for him. Not until they got across the city did he relax.

They made another stop and a handful of passengers boarded. Regulars, commuters going back and forth to work every day, talked to the driver. When they all sat down it got quiet again, except for one guy who took a seat up front and complained about his job to the driver. Andy didn't care and gazed at the fog rising from the river as they approached the onramp.

The first of the morning rush hour crowded the lanes, slowing them only a little. From his height, he could see inside the cars that passed beneath his window. Most of the passenger seats were empty. If something happened, if he couldn't get all the way to Virginia by bus or train, he could hitch a ride.

A laughing girl flashed in his mind, her slender throat golden in the sun as she threw her head back, hair glinting. Her dark lashes swept down and up as she touched his knee, her smile just for him.

Sarah.

Then the image vanished and they were at the train station. Nothing had changed in the last ten days—except him. The memory of a girl he couldn't know and a time he couldn't remember compelled him to get on a train and get back as fast as he could. What if he was brain damaged or psychotic or something? Why was that time all blacked out?

He hurried to purchase his ticket and find out when the next train to Newport News would leave. He could not get stuck in Maryland. The cops probably wouldn't think to look for him outside of the state. Since Marvin and Danny were in Germany, Aunt Lily wouldn't guess he'd go there anyway.

And he wasn't, he realized. He knew where to go.

Andy used the twenty minutes before his train to buy a sandwich, some drinks, and a bag of chips with the last of his money. When he came out of the restroom, the train had already arrived and boarding had begun. He knew he looked younger than seventeen, but he hoped anyway that they'd just take him for a college kid or something.

The attendant took his ticket, ripped it, and gave him back one-half without any more than a mumbled good morning. Andy pretended like he did this every day and made his way to a window seat. He sat down with relief and set the bag of food on the seat beside him, discouraging anyone from choosing to sit there. Conversation could be dangerous. What if he gave himself away to some granny lady or maybe blabbed to an undercover cop?

The train rolled out of the station around the time he'd run through accidentally talking to everyone from the Pope to Simon from *American Idol*. He leaned back and closed his eyes, trying to put everything out of his mind but his destination. Time always flew by when he thought of his father. What would his dad have thought of Marvin's Porsche?

One step closer to home, he thought. Andy slept and dreamed of souped-up cars and better days…

PART II

Andy Riley

CHAPTER 4

Truckload of Trouble

"Why can't I go?" Andy wanted to stomp his foot, but didn't. That would only make his mom angrier. "Dad said the company doesn't allow anyone under nine. I'm twelve now and school's out in two weeks."

"Not this summer," his mother, Nancy, said. Her hands were on her hips, not a good sign at all. "I mean it, Andy. Maybe next year."

"Next year! But Dad said—"

"I know what your dad said. He did not promise to take you this summer."

"But—"

"No buts. Now go get your shoes on. He's probably already at the yard waiting for us to pick him up."

"Aw, Mom! I'm gonna be forty 'fore I get to go." He stomped up the steps, knowing he'd lost. He wanted to cry but he was no baby. He was gonna be a teenager next year. Heck, he'd be driving his own semi in six. Then she'd see.

They got to the yard at the same exact time as his dad. Though he was still really angry with his mom, he could hardly wait to see him. The big man stepped down, a laundry bag slung over his shoulder like Santa Claus in June.

"Hey, Dad." Andy hurried to take the laundry from him. "I got it."

"Thanks, kiddo," he said. "Damn it's good to see you. I swear you get bigger every time I come home."

Andy grinned ruefully. "Yeah, tell that to Mom."His mom stepped between them, kissed his dad on the cheek, and said, "We need to talk, okay?"

Andy's smile fell and he turned back to the car, holding the heavy bag off the ground. Great, he thought, she'll talk Dad into leaving me behind, again. When they got back to the house, his parents went into the bedroom, with the door closed. He heard raised voices now and again, but nothing that dashed his hopes or gave him reason to believe Dad would tell Mom he would take Andy with him.

All through dinner and during the evening, he tried not to sulk, but it was hard because he knew his dad would never let him go if Mom put her foot down. Maybe if he could talk to his dad alone, convince him he would be fine, could even help him—then he might let him go.

On Sunday, his chance came when his dad asked, "Wanna go for a bike ride?"

"Heck yeah!" He ran to open the garage and they both mounted their bikes. "Should we do the trail or head to the park?"

"Let's go to the park," he said. "Race you to the stop sign!"

Andy pedaled hard, rising off his seat, the bike tilting side-to-side. His dad got there first, but not nearly by as much as he had before.

Winded, his father said, "Almost got me. You're getting fast."

"I ride a lot." Andy straightened on his seat as they

34

waited for the traffic to slow enough for them to cross. "I go all over, by myself. Sort of like you do, y'know? In your truck? Go all over? Like that, but I'm stuck here on my bike."

"Andy," his dad said in a weary voice. "You know how your mom feels about you going on the road with me."

"Yeah, but what about you? You said you'd take me as soon as I was old enough. Don't you want me to come with you anymore?" He waited, gut churning.

"Of course I want you to come, but when it's the right time," he said then nodded to the road. "All clear. What do you say we stop at the Dairy Queen before heading back?"

They pushed off, crossing together as Andy answered. "Yeah. Okay."

Being left behind really sucked, he thought, but it wasn't until his father was getting ready to leave Monday morning that he understood just how awful it felt. Even if he had school to attend that morning, and he was used to his dad being gone for weeks at a time, the disappointment of knowing he couldn't go with him this summer hit like a ton of bricks.

"Gotta take off, Andy," his dad said from the living room. "Come tell your old man goodbye."

Humiliating tears pricked his eyes and Andy dashed into the bathroom, afraid to cry and have his mom treat him even more like a baby. Why couldn't they see he wasn't a six-year-old anymore? He covered his face and tried to sniff back the flood wanting to escape.

His dad knocked on the door. "Andy? You okay? Can I come in?"

Quickly, he used the fancy pink and lace hand towel to wipe off his face. He said, "Come in."

"What's wrong, sport?" His dad leaned against the counter.

"Nothing," Andy said, curling the hand towel around his fingers. How embarrassing would it be to tell him he couldn't stand to be left behind another summer and it had made him *cry. "*Just jammed my fingers in the door."

"Ouch, let me see."

"No, I got it. It's okay."

He paused, watching him until Andy grew uncomfortable. "Okay. Well, your mom's gonna drop me off. I've got a short run this time around. Be back in a week, okay?"

Andy nodded and stood, accepting the brief hug without speaking—mostly because he didn't trust his voice.

The following Monday he got up as the sun rose. Four more days left of school. He could hardly wait. So it sucked that he couldn't go over the road with his dad *again* that year, but there would be lots to do that summer anyway. He dressed and wondered if his dad would be there for breakfast. Sometimes he left before dawn to get a jump on the morning traffic.

He made his way down to the kitchen. A clean spring breeze drifted in through all the open windows, bringing in the scent of his mom's flower bushes surrounding the house. Sunlight flooded the cheery yellow room, making the juice in the glasses so bright they could have come from oranges in heaven.

"Morning, honey." His mother set a bowl of cereal down. "Milk's on the table."

"Morning," he said, sliding into his seat, smiling at his dad and reaching for the gallon container. "You leaving today?"

His father nodded. "Yeah. I've been thinking about you going over the road with me. How about my next trip out?"

"Really?" Andy grinned huge and nearly overflowed his bowl with milk. He set the gallon down. "You mean it?"

His father smiled, eyes sparkling. "I wouldn't ask if I didn't mean it, kiddo. We'll be doing New York, thought you'd get a kick out of seeing the big city. What do you say?"

"Oh yeah!" His heart skipped a beat and he bounced in his chair. Wait until his friends heard. None of them were going to New York City he bet.

His mother leaned a hip against the counter and sipped coffee from a chipped mug. "Better not forget to do your chores or you won't be able to go."

She didn't sound happy and no way would he give her any reason to ground him. "Can I bring the camera I got for Christmas? Take pictures to show everyone?"

His dad stood, the chair scraping back from the table. He ruffled Andy's hair, as if he was still just a baby, and said, "You betcha. Your mom's gonna take me out to the truck now, but we'll talk more when I call tomorrow."

"Cool!" Andy could hardly eat his breakfast. He smiled as he watched his parents kiss.

At the door, his mom turned back. "Fifteen minutes, then you start walking, okay?"

He nodded. "I won't be late." Heck, he'd be early with such good news to share.

The rest of the morning passed in a haze of excitement. He planned to help a bunch and not get on his dad's nerves. Then maybe he could spend most of the summer out on the road with him. Everyone at school was jealous and by the time he got home, he had a whole bunch of kids that wanted souvenirs.

He was three feet inside the door before he noticed the house was dark, quiet, the drapes closed. Not even the kitchen light was on.

"Mom?" he called and threw his backpack on a chair. No one answered. "Mom?"

"I'm here."

Her voice was so low, so raspy, that he almost couldn't tell where it came from. Worried, he shuffled into the kitchen. She sat there, a full cup of coffee in front of her, the table littered with used tissues. When she looked up, her eyes were rimmed red, her nose bright pink in the diffused sunlight coming from the kitchen window.

"Sit down, Andy." Her forehead wrinkled and he noticed her hand trembled as she covered her mouth for a moment, as if she wanted to be sick.

"What is it, Mom?" His heart raced, his own voice sounding small and odd.

She laid her arm across the table, palm up in a plea for him to take her hand. Instinctively he did and her grip was hard.

Tears spilled down her face. "Your... It's ... I've been sitting here for hours trying to find a way to say this so ...

you'll be … okay… but I know… Listen, you've got to be very strong now. Can you do that, baby?"

He nodded, a lump already rising to his throat. "What's wrong, Mom?"

"Honey, your daddy had a massive heart attack this morning."

"Is he okay?" Andy could hardly breathe. "Did the doctors fix him?"

She shook her head. "No, sweetheart. He died before he got to the hospital."

He couldn't see. Tears blinded him. A great pain in his chest, in his gut, deep down inside him swelled to every inch of his body. He slid off the chair, unable to bear the weight of the grief. His mother fell with him to the floor, her arms wrapping around him as he wailed over and over again. They rocked together, sobbing, until the sun set and they were cloaked in darkness.

His dad's funeral was on a cloudy Friday afternoon. A lot of people came; all his father's friends and other drivers, bunches of people he didn't know. Even Aunt Lily came down from Baltimore, but she didn't look anything like she sounded on the phone. Heavy, her dress longer in front, she lumbered along slow enough a snail had time to get out of her way as she approached the grave.

He fidgeted in his formal clothes, the shirt scratchy, and the tie choking him. The preacher guy talked and talked, but mostly, Andy just held his mom's hand and tried to be strong for her, like she had told him to be that day in the kitchen. He cried though. Couldn't help it.

"Sorry for your loss," a trucker told Andy's mom after the funeral. He turned to him, "My names Frank. I worked with your pa. He said you were gonna go out on the road with him. If it's okay with your ma, I'll take you out. Just call and ask for Frank."

He didn't say anything. It felt wrong, like he was betraying his dad or something. It wouldn't be the same to go out with someone else and that made him want to cry again.

They didn't have many relatives. He didn't know what, but something bad had happened between his father and Aunt Lily years ago and she didn't even go back to the house after the cemetery. If there were cousins or uncles on that side of the family, he never even heard of them, let alone met them.

His mom's dad was around somewhere, but she always got all grim faced when his name came up so Andy didn't ask about him too often. He once heard her call him a *fingerless bum* but he never knew what that meant.

When the house emptied, she kicked her shoes off and leaned against a counter covered with bowls and pans of food. She hung her head, dark hair hiding her face. Andy went to her, wanting to be strong, wanting to be the man of the house and take care of her. Instead he cried on her shoulder, hugging her tight.

She was all he had left.

CHAPTER 5

Aftermath

Andy cried himself to sleep that night, and the night after that, and the one after that. His heart felt too big for his chest, as if it had swelled and bulged through his ribs. The ache never left. His mom worked so hard to keep from crying in front of him, trying to make things normal for them. But he'd been torn from normal and there was no going back now. He had to keep his grief to himself, make her think she was doing a good job putting the pieces of their life back together.

He totally missed the last days of school. Normally, that would have been a real treat, to get out a week earlier than everyone else would. Right now, he'd spend the whole summer at school if it would bring his dad back. He tried to tell himself life really hadn't changed all that much. After all, his dad was always on the road, always gone. Not like this was new. Except he wasn't ever coming home and he could never pretend that part away.

About a month after the funeral, the doorbell rang. Andy stood, leaning on his desk to look out his bedroom window. Gary's car sat in the drive. He and his wife had started coming around a lot lately, like they wanted to make sure they were all right. He wished they would just stay away. Gary was his dad's friend and it was weird for him to come over now. Like showing up at a friend's house when you knew they weren't home. Who did that?

He waited long enough to know his mom wasn't going to call him down and make him say hello, then slipped into the hall. Afternoon sun blazed brightly through the upstairs window, glazing the staircase like no other time of day. The rail warm and smooth beneath his hand, he stood silently and listened.

"I'm worried about him," his mother said. "He's taking it so very hard. Won't talk about it at all."

Like a broken record, she always whispered the three same words about him when she didn't know he could hear.

Withdrawn.

Quiet.

Depressed.

"I'll talk to him," Gary said with an authoritative finality, like he was already in charge of Andy's life. His mom didn't even stick up for him. She wanted to be saved from a difficult kid who just wouldn't get over his dad's death.

A slow burning rage built inside him. How dare she? How dare she let this man he had always hated try to take over for his dad? His father was probably spitting mad about this. Andy was his son and no one else would ever take his place.

He started down the stairs, ready to tell them they could all go find someone else to pity. He didn't want them. He didn't need them. They should just leave him alone. Why couldn't they just leave him alone?

Just then, the front door flew open and Gary's wife

hurried in, grocery bags in both hands. She smiled. "Hey, Andy."

He grimaced, uncertain now what to do. She acted all cheery and stuff. Why did she have to be nice?

"Hey," he answered lamely.

Her gaze met his briefly then turned to Nancy who stood in the hall. "I think I got everything you wanted. They were all out of that coffee you asked for, but I got some hazelnut instead. Hope that's okay."

"Its fine," his mother answered, stepping to take one of the bags from Janice. "As long as it has caffeine, it'll work."

Her wool sweater hid how thin she'd gotten. She spotted Andy on the stairs. "Why don't you come lend a hand?"

Her eyes dark, haunted pled with him to be okay, to go back to the way he used to be, to the kid he had been when he bragged about going to New York and promised everyone souvenirs. The kid who raced his dad to the stop sign. A son she could stop worrying about, stop caring about.

"I'm kind of tired," he mumbled.

The creases in her skin deepened as she frowned, aging her. "All right, hon, if you want to come on down later, I'll be here."

And so would Gary, Andy thought as he turned and went back to his room. But he was wrong about that because not five minutes later, a knock came at his door. Without getting up, he called, "What?"

"Can I come in?" Gary asked in a tone better used on four year olds—a creepy guy from the shadows offering to check for boogeymen under the bed or in the closet.

If he didn't let him in though, his mom would find out.

"Yeah, come in."

Gary opened the door, his brown eyes serious. Coarse black hair covered the backs of his hands, climbing up his wrists and disappearing beneath the cuff of his shirt. "You doing all right?"

As if doing all right was even a possibility. Andy just stared at him.

"Okay, I get it, dumb question." Gary smiled and leaned against the doorjamb. "You shouldn't stay up here in your room like this. It's not good for you. Come on down and hang out with us. We thought we'd do up some homemade pizzas. Sound like fun?"

Oh yeah, loads of fun, Andy thought. Janice and Gary were supposed to *help* and be *supportive,* but if anyone asked him, the best thing they could do was go away. Besides, what made Gary any kind of expert? He could hardly keep his own daughter out of trouble.

"For your mom, Andy." Gary tried. "Come down and help out."

Make me.

Gary stared determinedly at him. He didn't really care, Andy realized. He only cared about himself and looking like a hero instead of the zero he really was.

He seemed to recognize the shift in Andy and lowered his voice. "Look here kid, I know you lost your dad, but your mom's not doing all that well either. Stop being so selfish and start being the man of the house."

"Why?" Andy asked, his tone biting. "You're doing enough of that for everyone."

Anger tightened Gary's jaw. He took a deep breath. "If

you weren't so messed up, I wouldn't let you get away with talking to me like that. You remember your place and respect your elders."

"I thought I was 'sposed to play man of the house, now I'm just a kid. Make up your mind." He snarled, wishing he was grown and big like his dad so he could punch him in the face and knowing he would do nothing. Tears of rage choked him and he shouted, "Get out of my room!"

Screw him!

"What's going on?" his mom called, fear in her voice as she came up the stairs and stood outside of his door. "What did you say to him, Gary?"

"Nothing. I just said he should try to help around here more. It's not healthy for you to let him stay in his room all the time."

"He doesn't stay in there *all* the time." She sounded peeved.

Andy smiled inwardly, rubbing the dampness from his cheeks and chin.

Gary brushed long bangs out of his eyes. "You know, Andy you can talk to us, we're here to help you."

Gone was the angry guy from a minute ago. Here stood the yacht-man, the guy who could sell sand to desert people. A phony.

"We care about you, Andy."

His mom nodded. "I love you, sweetie. Gary knew your father very well. Talk to him when you need to. He's here for you."

What was he supposed to talk about? How wonderful it was to miss the trip with his dad? How awesome it had been to bury his father? Was he supposed to play games, watch movies, and have a good time with Jason next door as if nothing had happened? Maybe his mom was ready to hang out and have fun with her buddies, but he wouldn't be so disrespectful.

A knot squeezed tight in the bottom of his empty belly. "Can I be alone now?"

Gary exchanged a look with Nancy and said, "Give him time. It's only been a month."

Only a month. It had been a lifetime. Betrayed, cheated, and left behind, he wasn't supposed to lose his dad. Worst of all, he hadn't even gotten the chance to say goodbye. His dad died alone, all by himself without his family there.

Andy's mom held him briefly, kissed his forehead. "Come on down when you're ready, okay?"

He nodded and when her back was turned, glared at Gary. The door couldn't close fast enough on him.

Andy sat on the edge of his bed and tried to suck it up, tried to be the young man his father would be proud of. In a way, he wished he hadn't been such a good dad. Raised to be respectful, Andy wasn't like other kids his age. He didn't fight, or bully, or smoke, or do any of those bad things. He wished he did, because then the ache inside of him might go away.

He couldn't do that to his dad. He had to be the man of the house now. His dad would never curse Gary out, never beat him up. He had to be like that. Be good. Make his father proud and protect his mom.

As the days passed, Andy's mom faded away, like her

46

own shadow sucked her in, took away everything lifelike about her. She often sat in the darkened kitchen, an ever-living ghost of what once was. He found her there, after eleven on a hot, miserable August night.

She winced as he flicked the lights on, squinting at the sudden glare. Her raspy voice was a mere whisper. "Turn them off, Andy."

"Sorry," he said and turned them back off. Now he could barely see. Feeling his way to the fridge, he opened the freezer side door, thankful for the light as he hunted for an ice cream bar.

Behind him, his mother didn't say anything at all. Slender fingers wrapped around a coffee mug probably full of cold tea.

He asked, "You want some ice cream, Mom?"

She stared at him, stared longer, then asked, "What?"

"Ice cream," he said, offering her a smile, praying for one in return. "Y'know, that sweet yummy frozen stuff? You want one?"

She shook her head. "No…thanks."

Any other time she would have said it was too late for ice cream, that he should have finished his dinner, or that he would have to wait for breakfast. He took his time, standing with the freezer door open. She sat so still, he couldn't tell if she was even breathing. If it weren't for the occasional blink, he might have called 911.

The cold air felt wonderful against his overheated skin. She wouldn't turn the air on, saying she couldn't get warm and wasn't about to freeze to death just because he was hot blooded. That had been the most she said in days and hadn't said anything close to that much since.

She scared him.

"Mom," he said. "Why don't you go up to bed? Get some real sleep."

Without a word, she pushed the mug away, rose, and shuffled to the stairs. She climbed them slowly, her hair glinting in the bit of moonlight from the second floor window.

He put the ice cream back, no longer hungry, and closed the door. The darkness flooded back into the room. Shadows accused him of failing. He heard his father telling him he had to do better, be stronger, take better care of her.

The weight of it all made him want to drop to his knees, to just let the burden crush the life out of him. What more could he do? Instead of curling up and quitting though, he followed her up the stairs. She stood in the doorway to his room, staring at his empty bed. He held her shoulders, guiding her gently toward her own room, watching intently for a sign, a nod, even a look, anything at all to let him know she was okay. "I love you, Mom."

She sighed softly, lifting an arm, his father's bathrobe too big on her, yet she managed to touch the side of his face. "My Andy."

"Mom," he said, but she was already turning away, head bent, hair covering her face. He waited, made sure she got under the covers, then returned to his own room.

On his bed, he lifted the framed photo on his nightstand and propped it on his chest, as he had a thousand times. His mom had taken it the day they drove to Virginia Beach to meet him for dinner as he passed through on his way to

Mississippi. Standing beside his father, both of them smiling, Andy could clearly remember how perfect that day had been. A thin strip of aqua-blue ocean shone behind the bright red cab of the semi. He and his dad smiled as his mom snapped the picture. He could practically smell the ocean and remember how dusk brought a dampness that made him feel so close to the water.

What he wouldn't give to go back to that day.

Autumn came, and with it, school. From day one, Andy sensed a change in the way the other kids treated him. He walked among the scents of sharpened pencils, fresh notebooks, new leather shoes and their stares. They watched the kid who had lost his dad and never went to New York, never brought back any souvenirs. He was the kid without a father.

Shrill laughter echoed in the girl's bathroom and made him jump.

Not ready for this.

He breathed deep and counted door numbers in no real hurry to get to his homeroom. Kids he knew walked past him as if he didn't exist. He wasn't one of them anymore. He didn't belong there.

Good, he thought, forget them. What did he want with their fake sympathy anyway?

That lasted about half a second. He could hardly breathe. Class hadn't even begun, how was he gonna make it through an entire day? He kept his sweaty hands in his pockets, fiddling with the lint. Avoiding false condolences was easier than avoiding Larry Mathers, the school bully.

He stood smirking at the door to Andy's classroom.

Oh crap.

"Hear you're all talk, Riley. You got a big mouth, big claims of goin' to New York and all. You never went, did you? Big talker. You know what happens if you talk the talk—you gotta walk the walk. You walk the walk? Huh?"

All eyes on him, Andy froze.

My life is over.

"M-m-my," Andy stammered, meaning to say everyone knew it wasn't his fault, that his dad died and they couldn't go.

Larry twisted, pretending to be girly and in a high-pitched voice said, "M-m-m-m-my Toto, we ain't in Kansas anymore." He straightened as the kids snickered around him. "Should we start calling you Dorothy?"

Andy hung his head, face burning, wishing the roof would collapse or the floor give way or lightning strike him and put him out of his misery.

Mrs. Stitchen pushed through the mob of kids. "Larry Mathers, you stop this nonsense. Everyone get to class." She walked taller than the other teachers, books and folders squeezed to her hip. Wagging a finger in Larry's face, she said, "I'll see you after school, you hear me?"

He groaned. "I ain't done nothing!"

"I haven't done anything," she corrected. "But that's not true. No arguments or we'll see how many days Principal Carter wants to keep you in detention."

Larry slid into the room, shoulders hunched and Andy knew this would never end. For all the time he remained in this school, Larry Mathers would find any excuse to hurt and humiliate him.

His prediction proved true and for weeks he wove through the halls, doing everything he could to avoid running into Larry between classes. He walked a different way to school just in case. He went in by a different door and ate his lunch in a bathroom stall.

Some days he made it home without seeing Larry once, other days he wasn't so lucky. Never did he fight back though, not until health class one crisp fall day. Mrs. Stitchen rolled fake skeletons to the front of the room. The pair rattled on their separate poles. Standing between them, she asked, "What do you see when you look at these skeletons?"

Larry snickered. "Andy's dad!"

A blind rage rose inside him, collapsing his view to only Larry's fat, laughing face. He vaulted from his seat, going on instinct, freed from any self-control. Screaming furiously, he straddled Larry and punched him. "Take it back!" He punched him again. "Take it back!"

He barely noticed the kids yelling, "Fight! Fight! Fight!"

Hands grabbed his shoulders, but he shrugged free, voice hoarse with his screams. More hands grabbed him, wrestled him off the bloody boy on the floor. Breathing hard, he blinked. Kids stood, their eyes wide, horrified. Mrs. Stitchen and Mr. Wilkes from the room next door held him, even though he no longer struggled.

Larry moaned on the floor, his nose and lips smeared with blood.

Andy burst into tears.

"Andy," Mrs. Stitchen said." Andy, come on now."

Mr. Wilkes let go of him and bent down by Larry.

He let Mrs. Stitchen lead him away, avoiding eye contact with everyone. He couldn't stop crying, couldn't catch his breath and worst of all, he didn't know why.

Sobbing uncontrollably and embarrassed, he was forced to sit outside the principal's office to wait for his mother. The kids stared at him between classes, further humiliating him. By the time his mother left her new job as a newspaper editor and got to the school, he had settled down to intermittent hiccups. Like a baby, he thought with a grimace.

She didn't say one word, but breezed past him still smelling of clean air and colorful leaves. Now that her life got all straightened out and she had a job she liked, his life was falling apart. He listened intently, catching only the words *therapy* and *grief* and *suspension*. She would stick up for him, right? Take care of him like he took care of her?

"C'mon," she said, not pausing as she strode past him, expecting him to follow. "We can't afford a therapist for you right now, so you better straighten up."

He went numb, just cold everywhere. She didn't even want to hear his side of the story, didn't even ask if he was okay. She was mad. His mother never said another word about it and after that day, no one dared to say anything bad about his father again.

Her solution to all his problems was to sign him up for the soccer team. "It will be good for you to be around other boys your age. You can't spend the rest of your life playing video games in your room, hon." She flipped the enrollment forms, reading glasses at the tip of her nose.

Andy knew the truth though.

She wants me out of the house to work more hours.

"And it will help you move on." She added.

He hated that phrase *move on*. They said it a zillion times already. His dad wouldn't want him to argue though so he sighed in resignation. "I'll go, but I'm *not* staying if I don't like it."

"You can invite Jason, maybe he would like to watch you play sometime, or who knows, he might want to join."

Andy rolled his eyes. That would be a waste of time. Jason skipped gym class every week and bragged about it. "The Mitchell's can't afford it and Jason has a girlfriend now."

For two whole days he dreaded the first practice. Late coming in, all the other guys already knew each other. By the time he took the field, his stomach hurt. His mom got the best cleats and his jersey was bright white so at least the guys wouldn't give him a hard time for looking like a reject from a second hand store.

The coach stuck him in midfield, probably, Andy thought, because he didn't rate good enough to play fullback and he was too slow to guard the goal. That was the story of his life though, wasn't it? Never good enough to get a pat on the back, and never bad enough to have the cool factor of a rebel. Just a total geek wad.

Practice went okay. He didn't do great, but didn't do horrible either. Coach slapped him on the back and said, "You'll get 'em next time, boy."

Get who next time? Did they have a game already? He shuddered at the thought. Soccer was a tougher sport than he realized. All kicking legs and balls flying at your face and you couldn't touch it with your hands. He was just glad to have made it through alive. Standing to the side in the parking lot, not sure what to do or who to talk to, he tried to smile at a few of the kids, hoping they'd say hey or whatever.

No one did.

All of them were busy laughing and joking together and didn't even notice him. The parking lot began to empty as his teammates hopped into cars, minivans and one really cool super-wide pick-up truck that Andy thought ran on diesel gas—if he remembered right what his dad had told him.

Left alone in the dust of the last car, he started walking toward home. Not so far that he couldn't make it on foot, but far enough that by the time he got to the house, his feet hurt, and his legs were tired. He tossed his duffle bag on the floor, kicked off his sneakers, and called, "Mom, I'm home."

No answer. In the kitchen he found a note on the refrigerator.

Andy,

I left a dinner for you in the microwave. Heat for two minutes. Will be home as soon as I can.

Love,

Mom

He crumpled the paper and threw it away. Great, he thought, another meal all alone. While he waited for the food to heat up, he popped a can of soda and grabbed a fork. The microwave dinged and he sat at the kitchen table, in the silent house and ate the runny, cheap lasagna like he was supposed to.

The following Wednesday when she dropped him off,

he worked up the courage to ask, "You think you can stay, Mom? Watch me practice?"

She shook her head. "I've got to get back to the office. I'm taking my lunch hour late just to get you here on time as it is."

He knew that would be her answer. Retrieving the gym bag with his cleats and shin guards, he opened his door and said, "Whatever."

"Andy," she called, halting him before he got all the way out. "Don't do this to me. I've explained a hundred times I have to work the extra hours to make ends meet. Be a little supportive, okay?" She checked her watch, in a hurry to get going.

"Yeah, sure." Now he felt guilty. He promised his dad he'd watch out for her and here he was, mad about not getting a ride when she *did* work really hard. "See ya tonight."

On the field, some of the guys warmed up to him. They'd play their first game in a week and the coach had them all pushing extra hard to get ready. Andy even made a perfect pass that landed a goal. Parents watching from the stands stood up and cheered—for the guy who made the goal. There wasn't anyone there for him.

When practice ended, Andy didn't want to just stand around again, feeling like someone's discarded trash. He started across the parking lot, trying to avoid seeing fathers joke with their sons or moms pat their boys on the back. That ache settled heavier in the center of his chest again and he picked up the pace, eager to get away.

Vans and cars zipped by. None of his teammates looked

or waved at him. A Chevy minivan slowed down, the brake lights red in the shade of the late afternoon. He tucked the gym bag under his arm and hurried in the street toward the stopping van, a smile of thanks emerging on his face. But the van started again and as it took off, a kid gave him a curious look, as if he couldn't figure out what Andy was doing in the middle of the road.

Embarrassed, he hurried across like he'd meant to do that the whole time, even though his house was the other way. He waited until no one would notice, then backtracked and headed toward the house.

Miserable already, he wasn't surprised when icy autumn rain began to fall. He wouldn't be surprised if a huge boulder came down the street and broke every bone in his body at this point. If he had any luck at all, it was bad.

Cloaked in a hazy fog of loneliness he walked on, wondering if his dad was even paying attention up there in heaven. Water trickled through his hair, dripping down his neck, every drop on his bare skin stung, giving him goose bumps all over. Feet wet, he squished along in ragged sneakers, it sounded and felt no different than stepping barefoot in turds over and over again.

Andy turned onto Hiddenwood Lane and a car horn tooted behind him. He looked back through dripping bangs as his mom pulled up next to him. It almost made no sense to get in the car this close to home, but he opened the door anyway. He tossed the gym bag into the back and got in. The heater cranked on high, the smell of soggy foot-leather filled the car.

"When it started raining, I took off of work to give you

a lift. I'm sorry I missed you." She put the car in gear and drove the two blocks home. When he didn't talk, she said, "Let's get you inside and into some warm clothes, okay?"

He couldn't go back to the team again. He wouldn't go through all this again, watching dad's with their kids, getting stuck walking alone in the rain. No way did he need that in his life. As they walked inside and he headed up the stairs to change, he said softly, "I'm not going back."

Snow came and with it, a chill in the house that had nothing to do with the season. The hours Andy's mom worked and the early evenings changed them, distanced them. At Christmas, his mom insisted he wrap a red scarf around his throat, calling it cheery. He looked like a dork.

She kept her promise though and took him to the cemetery. The car stopped and they got out and as he had before, he counted the eighty frosted steps to his father's grave.

"It's snowing again." She held her free hand out, letting the flakes melt into the palm of her glove.

Like he cared.

She bent and leaned the cheap pine wreath against the marker. They used to come all the time, now they were no better than Aunt Lily, just saying a quick hello on major holidays.

She wrapped an arm around his waist, her head even with his for the first time in his life. "Your father was a great man with a good heart."

He stiffened. *A good heart?* Did she forget he died from a *bad* heart?

"Oh God, Andy, I'm sorry. I didn't mean it like that." She removed her arm and eased away.

They stood for a moment, almost like strangers now. He felt so crappy, like he was letting his dad down, but she didn't make it easy. Angry a lot, sad too much, she didn't laugh like she used to. Sure it wasn't easy being a single parent, but it was tough being a kid without a father too.

Honestly, all he wanted was to see his dad again. Opening gifts, alone with his mom, without his dad there, made him ill that morning. The idea of sitting down to a Christmas meal without his dad later on, made him sick. Putting up a fake tree and decorating it without Dad had been torture.

He was so over it all.

Alone in the cemetery with her, he didn't want to hate her for keeping him off the road with his dad for those three years he could have gone. He would never have that memory now, not ever. She couldn't wrap that up and stick it under the tree for him. But she had gotten him a big remote-controlled semi truck. Was it some kind of bad joke? Or did she really believe it was gonna make up for what she did?

It's not fair.

"Ready to go?" she asked.

"No." Was she crazy? Andy sniffed and shook his head. "We just got here!"

"Aren't you cold honey?"

"I'm not." He wiped his nose with his sleeve. "You can wait in the car, if you want."

She stomped her feet, breath pluming. "Didn't you wanna go see Jason? We better get going before it gets too late."

"Jason's busy with his family." Wind whipped into his ears and he hunched his shoulders, forcing the collar of his coat and the ring of his scarf higher to protect them. "All right, we can go."

On the way home, they didn't talk, which was nothing new. No matter how hard he tried take over the stuff his dad did around the house, it didn't make a difference with her. A part of him kept doing it because he thought his dad could be watching and would be proud his son made sure what needed fixing got fixed. But not his mom. She didn't notice anything but work and would likely be there now if they weren't closed for Christmas.

Without Jason, his life would just be one long fog of day in and day out, almost always by himself.

Jason once stood up for Andy and got beaten up instead. From that day on, they'd had a weird sort of friendship, Jason always treating him like he wasn't tough enough or something. Too bad he hadn't been in health class that day, Andy thought, he would have been shocked. Jason had a mouth on him that got him in trouble and Andy's mom wasn't a big fan of their friendship. She never stopped them from hanging out though. He changed his mind about going to visit Jason when they got home.

All the lights were off, his mom trying to conserve energy, and even with the Christmas decorations, the house looked vacant, like a family no longer lived there. "Can I call Jason? See if he can hang out for a while?"

"Finish your chores first. You won't be able to stay long, though; Gary, Janice and the girls are coming over tonight."

His mom dropped her purse in the hall and wearily made her way up the stairs to her room.

Andy rolled his eyes. A night with Gary and his family sounded like torture to him. He had never told his mom about what happened that summer they went to the concert, but he hadn't forgotten.

He took the trash out and ran the vacuum over the living room carpet, grumbling when it sucked up a portion of the Christmas skirt under the fake tree his mom had gotten on sale. They never had a fake tree when his dad was alive. She had complained about the mess and the effort it would take to water it regularly. He shoved the vacuum back into the closet, missing the smell of fresh pine almost as much as he missed his dad.

After he unloaded the dishwasher he called Jason, only to find out he had just left. While Andy's mom had made him do chores, Jason had gone off to some other kid's house. Andy thanked Mrs. Mitchell and hung up the phone, then sat on the couch, staring at the tree. A tree as fake as his life.

CHAPTER 6

Gary and Greensboro

Jason's parents, the Mitchell's were nice folks. When his dad died, they started inviting him to their vacation house in Syracuse. By the time Andy turned seventeen, he had turned them down four times. He didn't want to leave his mom even though she told him it was okay to go.

The summer before his senior year, he reconsidered. All of a sudden, his mom decided she was tired of being alone, wanted to meet new people and even went on a few blind dates, leaving him home alone even more often.

"I don't want you to go, Mom." Andy watched the frozen dinner she had bought him rotate in the microwave.

Adjusting the strap on a dress that was too low cut, she said, "I promised I wouldn't see anyone you didn't approve of, Andy. You can't expect me to spend the rest of my life alone. I need friends too."

"Whatever." The microwave dinged and he took the meal and a fork upstairs. She didn't try to stop him from taking food into his room, which was good because he didn't want to meet the guy taking her out. He stayed out of sight and watched her being picked up and later brought back from his bedroom window.

He liked none of his mom's dates, they were all either dorks, rednecks or nerds and when he ran out of those three options, he evaluated the car they drove and it was always a stupid choice. Nobody could replace his father.

"Last week of school and then we head out for Syracuse." Jason passed a crushed soda can between his feet. "I can't wait."

The sun warmed Andy's face as they walked home from school. He dreaded the weeks Jason would be gone. No plans of his own and his mom dating again, he foresaw a future of sitting bored to tears in an empty house with only daytime television to keep him company. That plain sucked. The can landed in front of Andy and he passed it back, thinking the few soccer practices he went to paid off as it went exactly where he intended. "Do you think your folks would still take me, after I turned them down so many times?"

Jason stopped in the middle of the sidewalk. "Dude, would you repeat that for me just one more time?" He twisted a finger in his ear, tilting his head. "'Cause I don't think I heard you."

Andy grinned and gave him a friendly shove. "You heard what I said."

Jason drew back and shot the can several feet up the sidewalk. "You sayin' you wanna come to Syracuse with us?"

"Been puttin' you off for years, I might just go for real this time."

"Yes! You gotta go, dude." Jason high-fived Andy. "It'll totally be a blast with you there. Don't even think of backing out now."

"I won't," Andy said, smiling but flipping out inside too. What had he just done?

"See ya," Jason said, backing up his driveway.

Andy gave him a quick wave and walked on to his house, already regretting his spur of the moment decision to go. His mom would be thrilled; he didn't have to worry about that. He still felt weird about leaving her on her own for all that time though. What would happen when he wasn't there?

The soft grass swallowed the sound of his steps as he cut across the front lawn. He stopped, surprised by the cars in the driveway. His mom wasn't at work, she was home.

The other car was the last thing he wanted to see.

Gary.

Six months ago, Gary got divorced, and now he was always at the house. Always. The front door opened with its all too familiar shudder and a long teeth-grinding squeal. Nothing a drop of oil wouldn't fix, but Andy hadn't had the time and Gary was good for just about nothing.

He kept talking about moving to North Carolina. He'd been promoted to manage a new branch of his company five hours away, some place called High Point just outside of Greensboro. Andy had never heard of it.

He couldn't wait for him to leave.

The scent of sun-warmed wood and Gary's leather jacket filled the hall. He dropped his book bag by the staircase. "Mom?"

"In here," she called from the kitchen.

Gary walked past the door and sat on the opposite side of the table.

Andy asked, "What's going on? Why are you home?"

"Gary showed up at the office and convinced me to take the rest of the day off. We're heading out to catch an early movie and dinner. I picked you up a TV dinner and you can order something off pay-per-view if you want."

"Well, have fun," Andy said and stormed out of the kitchen.

"Andy," she called, her chair scraped as she stood and came after him. She grabbed his arm. "What has gotten into you?"

He shook her off and lowered his voice, glancing back to the kitchen. As he thought he would, he found Gary watching them. Facing her, he said, "What do you *think's* gotten into me?"

She grabbed his arm again and pulled him into the living room. "He's not trying to replace your father."

"Like that's even possible," he said. At the pained look on her face he softened. "Why Gary, Mom? He's such a creep."

"No he's not." She straightened. "You never even gave him a chance. I don't want you giving him a hard time."

He rolled his eyes.

"I mean it." She sighed heavily. "He was there for us. The least you can do is show some gratitude."

Gratitude?

"Whatever, Mom. Just go have fun with your *boyfriend.* I'll stay here alone, as usual."

He brushed past her and went upstairs to his room. Offspring was loaded on his CD player and he flipped the volume up loud. If she didn't like it, she could just deal with it. He sat, then stood, full of pent up anger. He wanted to trash something, just rip something to shreds.

He picked up the alarm clock beside his bed and hurled it against the wall. It smashed, plastic flying everywhere.

Breathing hard, he listened for a knock at the door, his mom asking what he'd done and yelling at him to turn the music down. Instead, he heard, then felt, the front door open and slam closed. At his desk, he looked out the window.

Gary opened the passenger door for her then closed it gently after she got in. He glanced up, seeing Andy in the window. He frowned, glaring.

Andy gave him the finger. *Screw you.*

He waited there as they left, letting Gary know he wasn't going away, that he would be watching him. He understood his mom wanting to meet someone, heck he missed having a dad, wanted someone to teach him how to drive, be there. So he wasn't the only kid growing up without a father, but his dad didn't just live five miles away with a new wife. No, his was dead and wouldn't be coming to pick him up for weekend visitation.

He'd be damned though if Gary thought he could just move in and take over. Not Gary. Not ever.

Gary would be gone soon, moved away and his mom would find someone decent to date. Someone who wasn't a class-A jerk.

They took longer than normal to come home, the headlights shining through his darkened bedroom window at almost midnight. He crept into the hall. From his angle, he could only see their feet as they stood by the front door.

Gary said, "Think about it, okay?"

"North Carolina is so far away. I'm not sure Andy would be all right."

"You can't always be putting him first, Nancy. You got to think about your happiness too."

"But moving in with you? I'm just not sure yet."

"You know I'm serious. Come with me to Greensboro."

Andy held his breath and leaned far enough over so he could see his mother's face. She wouldn't move. No way. She had promised his dad they would spend the rest of their lives in this house, grow old here.

"Think about it," he repeated.

"I will," she whispered as he bent and kissed her, full on the mouth.

Andy stormed into his room and slammed the door behind him.

No!

They weren't moving and not with Gary of all people. How could she even consider it? How could she *kiss* him like that? In their house. In his dad's house!

She knocked on the door. "Andy?"

"Just go away!" He was not going to give her the chance to tell him they were moving or that she was going to marry the worst guy on earth.

* * *

For the whole next day he refused to speak to his mom until dinner. "I'm going with the Mitchell's this summer."

If he was in Syracuse, they couldn't move. If they couldn't move, then she couldn't be with Gary. Simple. Gary was going to be out of their life for good.

"Okay," she said and sipped her coffee.

Not a real reaction at all. No, she saved that for when she called Gary after the dinner dishes had been cleared from the table.

"It might be good for Andy to get away for the summer." She tried to speak low, but he heard her anyway. "I don't know. Yeah, I'm still thinking."

He thought she'd agreed too quickly. Even though she had always encouraged him to go, now with Gary in the picture and the whole Greensboro thing, he expected some kind of argument. Knowing her, she would bring this back up when he least expected and try to talk him out of going. Maybe she'd offer a deal to take him somewhere cool just to tempt him into canceling with Jason.

It wouldn't work.

Andy waited all the next day for her to come to him, but she never did. Maybe she *wanted* him to go away so she could get closer to Gary? Oh God, why hadn't he thought of that?

By the last day of school, two days before he left with the Mitchell's, the tension between him and his mom had eased. His fear that he had given her a chance to move behind his back felt almost silly now. She wouldn't do that to him, he realized. Gary stayed away much of the week and that helped a lot too. Guess he had a lot of packing to take care of, Andy thought happily.

"No school for three months mom." He sat at the kitchen table.

She finished rinsing the lettuce before responding.

"There's something I want to talk to you about."

"Is it about my trip? I'll be fine, Mom, really." He figured, from the serious expression on her face, she wanted to say something about Gary but he didn't want to hear anything about him.

She let out a deep breath like a deflating balloon.

This is it, he thought.

"No, it has nothing to do with the Mitchells. I've been meaning to talk to you about this for a while, I just didn't find the right time to bring it up, but we have to talk before you leave."

Andy interrupted his mom, playing it off like he didn't have a clue what she meant. "Mom if you don't want me to go I won't, the Mitchells will understand." He added, "Or you could take off from work and come with us; it will be fun, the Mitchells have plenty of space in their house. I've seen pictures."

She didn't look up from tearing the lettuce into a glass bowl. "I'm going with Gary to North Carolina to look at houses."

The floor buckled beneath him. His ears buzzed. "Are you saying we're moving in with Gary?"

"No, we're just looking. Gary needs to find a place down there and he would love for us to live with him, but for now I'm only helping him." She finally looked up, the concern in her eyes unfair.

He wanted her to be angry or mean or anything but worried because then he couldn't shout at her, refuse to allow her to go. Tears pricked his eyes and when he spoke, his voice cracked. "Mom you promised, you promised Dad you would grow old here."

"Yeah I know," she said, drying her hands on a towel. "But that was a long time ago. Andy, please understand; he died right after we bought this house."

"So? Does that break your promise to Dad? Didn't he mean anything to you at all?" He hated it, but he started to cry. Almost a man and he couldn't keep from crying.

Tears trekked down her face, too. "I loved your father, Andy. I will always love him, he was my husband, but he would want us to live happy lives. Your father loved you very much; he loved you so much. I know you're still hurt. I was hurt too, I was very hurt... We have to move on even if the pain never goes away. I will never forget your father and nobody can ever replace him, that doesn't mean we can't be happy."

All along Andy thought he had figured it out, had made it so she couldn't move. Now he saw that had done more harm than good. He'd lost. "Then tell me why Mom? We're happy here. You like your job. Jason and I are friends. Why now?"

She went to him and put a hand to his cheek. "It's not the same. It hasn't been since he died. Living here is painful for me, for both of us. We can have a fresh start."

He pulled back and wiped his face. "We can hang out more often Mom. I'll be good; I promise I'll be good. I won't go with the Mitchells." Desperate, he offered his best compromise. "I won't even mind if Gary visits on weekends."

She put a hand on his arm. "It's not that, Andy and just because Gary said he wants us to live with him doesn't mean it's what we're doing. We were only talking about the possibility."

In her gaze, he saw finality. She must have known about this all along.

"You already decided, didn't you? You're not asking me anything. You're just telling me!" He pushed her away. "It's Gary, isn't it? It's always been about Gary. You don't care about me anymore. I'll bet you're happy I'm going away, aren't you Mom?"

She wiped her tears. "Andy, please understand… Gary was there for me. Don't walk away angry, we need to talk."

He rushed to his room. Behind the closed door he sat on the edge of his bed. He felt like his dead alarm clock, all broken and unable to function anymore.

I hate her.

He pressed his palms hard against his eyes. In that sparking red blackness, he saw his mom in a wedding dress, marrying Gary. He carried her over the threshold of their new house in North Carolina, a small and hideous thing with a room for Andy half the size of the one he had now. He pictured them laughing in his face and Gary demanding Andy call him Dad.

He wept like a kid again.

CHAPTER 7

Off to Syracuse

Andy slept little over the next two nights. He and his mom didn't speak, mostly because he avoided her. Once she left for work, he'd leave his room and he made sure to be hanging out over at Jason's around the time she came home. The nights were tricky, he had to time it just right, wait for her evening shows to start, come in, grab something fast from the kitchen, then flee up to his room.

On the morning they were to leave for Syracuse, he woke feeling like he couldn't go unless he made everything okay between him and his mom. She did have a right to be happy, just like he did. In January he would turn eighteen and had already thought about getting his own place next summer, and here he was, flipping out because she was thinking about moving.

Gary.

All because of him. Why him? Every time he wanted his mom to be happy he had to deal with Hairy Gary, the big dumb ape. He was right about that though. His mom deserved so much better than that jerk.

He didn't want to apologize outright, he wasn't totally wrong after all. The best way to say sorry, he thought, was to simply put his tail between his legs and be super nice. This usually worked well.

He got out of bed, too excited about the trip ahead to sit still. He dressed, noticed his mom's closed door, which meant she was sleeping in. Good. She worked too much lately. He left her asleep and headed out the front door.

Already the Mitchells were loading the station wagon. Neighbors washed their cars, cut their grass, and walked their dogs. The old lady across the street, the one his mom once thought died because no one had seen her for a while, trimmed her rose bushes. The entire street had come out, almost as if they wanted to celebrate the Mitchells departure. Heck, the neighborhood might throw a block party after they were gone.

Mrs. Mitchell came out of the house carrying a cooler.

"Need some help?" Andy asked.

Beneath her ankles, flip-flops dug deep into the dying grass with each step she took, then *thwapped* her heel. Pearls of sweat raced from her temples. "You can get the passenger door for me, sweetie."

The Mitchells were the black sheep of the neighborhood, often accused of being loud, rude, and low class. Most everyone kept a safe distance. They were harmless though, or his mom would never allow him to go on such a long trip with them.

Andy gently pulled the door open, afraid to tug any harder and make it pop off. The Mitchells might be safe, but he wasn't so sure about their station wagon.

"Thank you dear." Mrs. Mitchell set the cooler in the floor of the old wagon, making the tail end dip a good two inches.

Holy cow, she had to be strong. "You're welcome."

Mr. Mitchell came from behind the house with a fishing pole. "This is Jason's old pole. He's rough on 'em and tore it up pretty good, but I got it working. Thought you'd like to have it."

"Wow," Andy said, accepting the pole. "Thanks."

Mr. Mitchell wiped sweat from his forehead. "Not a problem. You're gonna need it up there."

Andy couldn't wait to see the house in Syracuse. Jason talked nonstop about nearby Onondaga Lake and the trout as big as cars and catfish as big as sharks. He talked about the girls and campfires on its shores. Although he knew Jason exaggerated, he still wanted to see for himself.

The Mitchells couldn't seem to get a grip on anything this morning. Jason was still packing and Mrs. Mitchell, curly blonde hair sticking up, her hefty stature not slowing her one bit, ran around the house forgetting what she intended to do. Andy hid his laughter as he watched them.

Jason came out of the garage with more fishing poles and started stabbing them into the already overloaded car. Mr. Mitchell, his dark hair stuck to the sweat on his round face, tinkered under the hood of their ancient white station wagon, checking oil and water then banging his head on the hood latch when he straightened.

Total chaos.

They wanted to hit the road in thirty minutes, but it didn't appear they were anywhere near ready to leave.

"Is it all right if I stop home for just a minute? I forgot something," Andy asked.

Mr. Mitchell nodded and took his backpack. "If you aren't back by the time we leave, I'll honk for you at your place to come out."

Andy thanked him and walked home, preparing himself to say goodbye to his mom. This was not going to be easy.

He opened the front door, a prickle in his eyes already. Three long weeks he wouldn't see his mom. Eleven hours away from each other. Farther than they'd ever been. Not like he could holler and she would appear.

In the house, he didn't see her. With little time left, he impatiently shouted, "Mom, where are you?"

"I'm upstairs."

He found her packing in her room. "You're getting ready for North Carolina?"

"Yeah Gary and I want to leave after we get off work tomorrow. I want to be ready, don't need to wait until the last minute." She perked up, responding to his easygoing tone and he smiled.

"I hope you have a nice trip."

"You, too."

"*My* stuff's already loaded in the Mitchell's car." Andy smiled.

She smiled back, folding a top. "Well smart ass, then you should help me pack."

Andy grinned. "I'm about to leave Mom, you're on your own."

She chuckled and grabbed a pair of rolled up socks. "Help, or I'll throw these at you."

"I dare you." Andy laughed as he ducked too late and the socks caught the side of his face.

"Thought I'd lost my aim, didn't you?"

"Okay, you got me this time, but wait until I get back.

Revenge is sweet." He picked up the socks and handed them to her, turning serious. "So you like Gary?"

"After all he's done for us, don't you think the least I can do is help him now? I'm going to help him get settled in down there, that's all. Maybe someday it'll become more, but I'm not ready and I know you're not either."

"You don't have to explain, Mom." His cheeks warmed.

"I know, but I want you to know before you leave. Don't worry about anything. Most important is that you have a good time. You deserve to have fun and you haven't been anywhere for a while. Don't worry about your mom." She closed the suitcase.

"I'll miss you."

"I'll miss you too. I'll call you every day," she said in a soft voice.

A weak, asthmatic horn honked outside. Andy stepped to the window and parted the curtain. "They're here."

His mom followed him down the stairs and outside. She walked straight to the passenger door to speak with Mrs. Mitchell. "You have all my contact information, right?"

"Yes, Mrs. Riley. Don't you worry about a thing. He'll be just fine."

She stood as a sudden wind gusted through her dirty-blond hair. She tucked the locks away from her face like she has done a million times and said to him, "So this is it, handsome. Did you pack your jacket in case it gets cold?"

The funny feeling in his gut moved to his throat and he just nodded.

Tears glinted in her eyes as she reached for him. "Okay then, give your mom a hug."

They embraced each other like they hadn't done in a long time and that uneasy feeling in Andy's throat reached his eyes. He barely kept himself together as his mom finished with a little kiss and let him get into the car. He slammed the heavy, unwilling door shut.

The old engine grinded to a start, a puff of smoke exited from somewhere under the car. Belts screamed for mercy as Mrs. Mitchell waved goodbye through the open passenger window. They slowly rolled away from the curb.

He leaned out of the window and waved. "Love you, Mom."

She waved from the sidewalk with a forced, happy look on her face. "Love you too, Andy!"

He kept looking out the window until he couldn't see her anymore.

Jason grinned and said, "Dude, are you crying?"

Andy kept his face turned toward the window, letting the draft dry his tears as he tried, and failed to ignore him. "Just got something in me eye."

"Whatever you say, buddy." Jason put headphones on, closed his eyes, and leaned back. "I'm gonna chill for a while."

The car remained quiet until they hit the interstate and Jason's parents argued about which route had the least amount of construction to slow them down. Jason sang to the music only he could hear on his IPod.

Andy daydreamed.

CHAPTER 8

Watercolor Memories

They hit a steady speed, the tires rumbling along the highway in a lulling hum. Andy dreamed of water. Great, wonderful waterfalls crashed into a wide lake, the mist casting wavering rainbows across an expanse of green foliage. He curled his toes into sand as soft as silk, warm, inviting. A girl he'd once watched at school, fascinated by the way her gold hair spread against tanned, bare arms walked toward him along the shoreline. She wore a white and pink bikini and a smile to match.

He imagined his own yacht by the pier and it appeared, stately and huge beneath a setting sun. All his friends, dozens of them, came to visit. Servants prepared the finest foods for a bonfire they would light when night fell.

Andy.

A familiar voice traveled on the warm breeze to him. His dad waved at him from the balcony of a gigantic mansion. His mom wore a straw hat, protecting her from the sun as she worked in a huge garden.

Larry, the kid who picked on everyone, wore a hot catering suit and brought all his friends drinks. Others from school like Larry waited on everyone they ever picked on. They could only speak when spoken to and they could only answer with, "Yes, very well, sir."

Even Jason was there, fishing off a boat in the lake. He reeled in one catfish after another and they were all as big as sharks, just like he always said.

Andy sipped his ice cold drink and leaned back in the chair. *Paradise*. This was the life. His happy smile softened, faltered, as a female voice whispered softly, drifting under the rush of the waterfall. A sad voice, he listened, but couldn't understand. The voice grew louder. His mom. She repeated the same words over and over again. "*You have to be strong now, Andy. You have to be strong.*"

He twisted to look behind him and his mom no longer stood in the garden. There was no garden, no mansion, no yacht—everything was all gone. Only Jason remained on the boat, trying desperately to get his attention.

"Andy, wake up. Wake up wake up!"

His mom was gone and his dad was gone too. Not again. *Not dad, not again.*

"Mom—Dad!" Andy shouted and opened his eyes.

Jason laughed. "Dude, it's me Jason, are you in a coma or something? I've been trying to wake you up forever. Are you okay?"

"Was I asleep? Where's my drink? I dozed off I guess."

"Dozed off my butt," Jason said, "you were asleep for hours. We're on the freeway just outside of Scranton, Pennsylvania. You slept like a hibernating bear and you weren't drinking anything."

"I must have been dreaming."

"I'll say."

"Would you like some cold water, Andy?" Mrs. Mitchell asked, holding up a small dripping bottle from the cooler on the front seat.

"Thanks." Andy took the bottle. "How far are we?"

Mr. Mitchell looked at him in the rearview mirror. "We're more than half way."

Andy drank then closed his eyes, hoping to return to his fantasy world and his mom and dad. The great crash of the waterfall hitting the lake sounded right beside him. He tilted his head and peeked. Wind drafted through a worn rubber door gasket. He tried to go back to the beach, but now that he knew where the sound came from, he just wanted to rip the rubber out and forget the whole thing. Driving to Syracuse was a drag. He was glad that he slept away a few hours.

Jason initiated a game of making up stuff to go with the license plates they passed. Like 5T1-KZY, became five tons of crazy. The game got old though and Andy's attention slipped to each semi they passed. The dream had been so real, so distinct. Had his father ever been on this freeway?

They stopped a few times for food and gas, but got right back on the road. The sun fell below the horizon, reflecting purples and hot pinks along the base of a cloud line. Reds and oranges eased into a hot yellow where the sky met the earth. The most brilliant sunset he could remember. He thought of waking Jason, telling him to check it out, but didn't. Maybe Jason would think he was dumb for waking him up from what might be an awesome dream just to look at the sky.

Well after one a.m. Friday morning, they finally arrived in Syracuse. Jason had been asleep in the car for hours. Tired as a dog, Andy unfolded his cramped limbs and got out of the car. To his relief, the Mitchells decided not to unload everything. They brought in what they absolutely needed and left the rest.

In the dark, he could barely see the house for all the trees surrounding the place. Inside, closed windows and proximity to the lake gave everything a damp, musty scent. Mrs. Mitchell opened a few windows and the stuffiness went away on a clean, cool breeze. He followed the family up the stairs where she opened more windows.

"The bathroom's right through there," she said quietly to Andy as Mr. Mitchell nudged Jason toward another room. "You boys will sleep in there. You should be good until morning."

"Thanks," he said, easing past Mr. Mitchell to find a pair of twin beds, Jason already sound asleep in one. He toed off his shoes and got beneath the blankets. He waited for sleep to come.

Uncomfortable in an unfamiliar room, he lay wide-eyed, watching the pattern of moonlight and tree branch on the ceiling. He hadn't slept in any other bed than his own since before his dad died. His eyes adjusted to the darkness and defined the furniture, the curve of Jason's shoulder across from him. He wanted to talk, to whisper late into the night about nothing and everything, but there was no one to talk to. For a long time he lay awake until sleep finally claimed him.

A clatter from somewhere downstairs woke him the next morning. He dressed and went to explore the noise. On tiptoe, he headed into the kitchen where Mrs. Mitchell fixed breakfast.

"Good morning Andy, how did you sleep?" Her cheery smile was way too big for this early in the morning.

He yawned. "Good I guess. Where's Jason?"

"Normally, he stays up half of the night and it takes an act of God to get him out of the bed in the morning. Today he got up before I did, not sure what's gotten into him. Maybe he fell out of bed," she joked. "He's in the living room. I hope you're hungry, how do you like your eggs?"

The thought of eggs twisted his guts, but he didn't want to be impolite. Not much for breakfast food at all, he almost always skipped the meal. "Sunny-side up, please."

"And he says please," she said, laughing and shaking her head. "Now there's something Jason could learn from you."

He could hardly wait to get out of the house and see the sights. He peeked through the open door. Jason slept on the couch, the TV on.

"Is he asleep?" Mrs. Mitchell asked.

"Yeah, looks like he's pretty out of it."

"Breakfast is ready." Mrs. Mitchell yelled loud enough to wake up the entire town.

Andy sat down at the dining room table. He didn't know where to start, there were three eggs and a mound of bacon on his plate. He poked at the food, a bit of raw egg white jiggling along a river of yellow yolk.

Jason came in and sat down. As soon as Mrs. Mitchell disappeared into the kitchen, Jason pulled him out of the chair, pointing at the fishing rods stacked by the screen door.

"She won't care," he whispered as Andy hesitated.

Eager to escape the runny yolk, Andy hurried to get his

shoes and meet him at the back of the wagon. They picked two of the Mitchell's bicycles, collected the tackle box, and rode to the nearby lake. Jason knew his way around and Andy pedaled right behind him. They left the road to take a shortcut through the woods created by a zillion bicycles over the years.

He followed bravely, despite the difficult path and the branches that scraped his arms and face. Twice he had to push his bike up a steep incline because he didn't have enough momentum, unlike Jason who knew when to speed up enough to clear each one.

Screw fishing, he thought, overtaken with the thrill of hitting the smaller hills hard enough to get airborne. He could ride his bike all day. This was *normal* for Jason, he thought as they reached a crest and his friend stopped. He halted beside him.

Below them lay a humongous lake. The water looked as still as glass and reflected the blue sky and white billowy clouds perfectly, almost as if he could see the sky in China looked exactly the same.

"This is my secret spot. The fish bite here by the dozens." Jason hopped off his bike and started across the sand.

He had forgotten why they came. The trees, so very many of them, circled the lake, the cool shadows between their ancient trunks promising sights he'd never find back home.

"Well, come on," Jason said. "We've got all day, but I wanna spend it fishing, okay?"

"Comin'," Andy called with a grin. He pushed his bike

along on the sand and left it lying beside the other.

Jason expertly assembled the fishing gear and showed Andy how to use it.

Andy whipped the pole like Jason had, but his hook splashed down practically right under his pole.

"Not like that," Jason said, impatient. "Here, watch."

He cast the bait far into the lake and grinned. "Like that."

Andy tried again, and this time he released too soon and the lure landed in the sand behind him.

Jason rolled his eyes. "Dude, it ain't rocket science."

"Give me a minute. I'll get it," he said with determination. His next was better and by noon, he was proud of himself. The casting thing wasn't so hard once you got the timing down. Only one drawback so far that he could see.

Neither of them caught a single fish.

Andy joked, "Your secret spot isn't all that great."

"Probably 'cuz it's too early yet," he said wisely. "We should move further north, where they hang out until mid summer."

Andy suspected Jason knew just as much as he did where the fish were-not at all, but he was happy to push his bike along and see more of the lake. He should have come a lot sooner, like every year. This was so much better than he thought. He liked that there really weren't any people. No teachers to worry about, no kids to avoid. Just relaxing, for like the first time in forever.

"There!" Jason pointed to an abandoned pier. "Bet there's tons over there."

After half an hour, Andy asked, "You getting hungry?"

"Starving," he said and pulled a mangled chewy granola bar from his pocket. "Wanna share?"

Anything would do at that point and he nodded. He wished they would have packed a real lunch. If they came back again, and he hoped they did, they'd bring real food to eat.

"Hey, think you got one there," Jason called.

Andy's line zinged out and Jason talked him through reeling in his first catch. The itty-bitty carp didn't put up much of a fight.

"Dude," Jason said, laughing. "You caught bait!"

He chuckled despite his embarrassment. "Hey, at least I caught *something.*"

"Don't rub it in," Jason growled. "We must just be early or something."

They fished until sunset, never catching anything big enough to keep. The ride back home seemed to take much longer, as hungry and tired as he was, but he didn't care. "This is awesome. We have to come back tomorrow."

Visibly honored, pride poured off Jason in buckets. "Definitely. Second day's always the best anyway. We'll get one of them big catfish tomorrow, I bet."

Andy nodded, beaming as he coasted into the yard, more comfortable on the bike now that he'd logged so many hours on it. Wait until mom hears about this, he thought. She might even try to come up for a little while to see it herself.

Mr. Mitchell sat on the back deck, relaxing in a chair. "What, no fish?"

Jason shook his head. "Not today."

"Second day's always better," Mr. Mitchell said as the boys went inside.

Andy kicked his sandy shoes off by the door. "Mrs. Mitchell, can I call my mom?"

"Go ahead, hon. We'll be firing up the grill in a few minutes, so you've got time before dinner." She tapped her flip-flops, popping the backs against her heels.

"Thanks." He lifted the receiver from the wall and punched in the numbers for his mother's cell phone. After four rings it went to voicemail. He hung up and dialed again, thinking maybe she couldn't dig the phone out of her purse in time. When the recorded voice asked him to leave a message again, he asked her to call back.

Life had taught him to worry. Bad things happened just when you thought everything was normal. All night he kept trying, kept waiting for the phone to ring. She had promised to call him every day, yet as he ate dinner he didn't remember, the night grew loud with insects and the sky passed from purple to star spangled, the phone didn't ring.

"I'm sure it's all right, Andy," Mrs. Mitchell said as they escaped the biting mosquitoes and went inside. "Maybe she forgot to charge the phone."

"Maybe," he mumbled.

They all went to bed and Andy tried to sleep, but Jason kept talking about how big the catfish would be.

"I bet we get a two-footer. Maybe bigger."

Andy mumbled agreement, not really listening.

"You think we got a strong enough line? I'll have to ask Dad in the morning if he's got anything stronger than twenty-pound test."

"Okay," he said, tucking his hands beneath his head.

"I bet if we leave right before dawn, we could get them coming up for breakfast. Fish eat breakfast, right? I read somewhere that they sleep with their eyes open because they don't have any eyelids. That would be weird hey? To sleep with our eyes open? Or maybe even more weird not to have eyelids."

From the other bedroom, Mrs. Mitchell called, "Go to sleep, Jason!"

"'Kay, Ma," he called back, then chuckled and whispered, "she'll be asleep in like a minute."

But they stayed quiet anyway, Andy too freaked to be up for much chatter.

Distant thunder rumbled and a drop of rain splattered on the windowsill beside his bed. He waited, expecting to feel a fine spray from the impact, but none came. The screen and distance left him dry. To keep his worry at bay, he counted the raindrops as they started.

Twenty-three...twenty-six...thirty-eight...

He lost count as the deluge came. He fell asleep to Jason's last words.

"I hope it doesn't rain tomorrow."

CHAPTER 9

No Escape from Nightmares

Andy woke up from a horrible nightmare as booming thunder filled the room and lightning threw everything into sharp relief. Covered in sweat, he breathed hard and rubbed his eyes. The clock on the table read 12:22 a.m. and beyond it, Jason snored like a table saw.

He lay down and stared at the sky unable to shake the awful feeling that something terrible had happened. He listened for the phone to ring, for his mom to call and say everything would be okay. Sleep didn't come easy.

The next morning, Jason dragged him back out to the lake. Tired now, and not feeling right, the magic of the day before disappeared. Everything was wet from the rain and riding through mud exhausted his legs. They ran out of bait by ten and there wasn't a single fish in the bucket. It didn't matter. His heart wasn't in it anymore.

"Stop worrying, dude. I'm sure she'll call tonight, no biggie." Jason didn't sound sympathetic, he sounded annoyed, like Andy was ruining his vacation.

He sort of felt like he was.

"Hey," Jason said. "Let's go for a swim!"

Andy wanted to go back, try again to call his mom now that it was midmorning and she would surely be awake. He stood there, barefoot. Maybe Gary kept his mom so busy that she had forgotten to call him like she promised. That had to be it, he thought. When she finally called he was gonna let her know how ticked off he was.

"C'mon." Jason splashed him. "Don't be a chicken. *Bawk, bawk, bawk!*"

The water felt warm and good. He rolled his eyes and took off his shirt. "All right, I'm coming."

What if she called while he was swimming? Well, that would be her fault for not keeping her promise. Besides, she couldn't expect him to sit inside all day waiting on her. His shirt half up, he stopped as the Mitchell's station wagon pulled up on the gravel road above the beach.

Mr. Mitchell got out of the car and walked toward the pier. No fishing pole in his hands, he stopped by Andy. He lowered his head, toying with the car keys.

Andy asked, "Mr. Mitchell, are you okay?"

"Dad what are you doing here, is something wrong?" Jason pulled himself up onto the pier.

Mr. Mitchell just stared at them, eyes grim and unable to meet Andy's for more than a moment.

Something's wrong, Andy thought and started shaking, his heart beating fast.

"You boys need to load the bikes in the wagon. We have to get back to the house and get Andy packing."

"Why does Andy have to leave?" Jason asked as he started to gather their things.

Andy put his shoes back on, but couldn't bring himself to ask what he was afraid to know.

As they loaded their bikes in the back, Jason asked, "What's going on? Andy's supposed to stay for the whole time. Why does he have to go now?"

"Just do what your dad says." Andy spoke harsh, surprising himself. He didn't want to hear whatever had made Mr. Mitchell look at him that way. He especially didn't want to know if it had anything to do with his mom. That same panicky feeling deep in his gut came back.

Can't this all just be a bad joke? Please?

But nobody was laughing. Mr. Mitchell got in the car while the boys closed the tailgate. He ordered Jason to sit in the back seat and Andy in the front. The station wagon left a plume of rocky dust behind them. The rear tires squealed, filled the air with burnt rubber as they made contact with the paved road.

"Andy." Mr. Mitchell paused briefly, not taking his eyes off the road. "You must be very strong now."

He went cold, like ice flowed in his veins. "Is my mom okay?"

Knuckles white on the steering wheel, he said, "She's been in a car accident."

"But is she okay?" Pain stabbed his ribs as he inhaled, waiting for the answer.

"You'll be on the next flight home." He turned the blinker on, slowing only slightly as he hurried them back to the house. "It's all been arranged. Someone will pick you up at the airport there."

"What happened?" Andy choked the question again. He didn't care what was arranged or where he was going. "Where's my mom?"

Mr. Mitchell waited almost until they were back to the house to answer. "I only know that a truck hit your mom's car in the fog last night."

He couldn't speak. The world swam around him. He should have gotten the police looking for her when she didn't call, should have known she wasn't all right. "She's not...okay, is she?"

He didn't answer at all. Mrs. Mitchell waited outside with his backpack and the bag of clothes he'd brought. She had tears in her eyes as she got in the car. "I packed your things, Andy. We'll get you back as fast as we can."

Jason asked, "Is his mom all right?"

"We don't know, honey." Mrs. Mitchell didn't say more and Andy couldn't ask.

They drove straight to the airport. The entire time Andy tried to convince himself she was fine, just busted up some, laid up in a hospital. He could even get her a book or something to read. She liked to read.

The tears came and he turned to the window, hiding them from Jason, who didn't make jokes this time. No one spoke until we pulled up to the United terminal at Hancock International.

Mr. Mitchell said in a small, quiet voice. "Ya'll go and check Andy in. I'll park the car and come find you."

Andy followed Jason and Mrs. Mitchell through the automatic door and into the airport. His head hurt, bouncing toward his worst fears and then dancing away as a flood of new experiences hit him. Never in an airport before, it looked very different than he expected. White everywhere, gleaming metal and signs along wide walkways spread in direction that didn't seem to have any rhyme or reason to them.

Mrs. Mitchell had to pay fifteen extra dollars to have his duffle bag of clothes checked in. He watched tons of people hurrying to get somewhere other than here. He knew the feeling, despite the guilt of insuppressible excitement warring with his dread.

Mom, be all right. Be all right.

"Hey, what kind of plane you goin' on?" Jason asked as the dark haired girl typed on her computer. "I bet it's one of those big jumbo bus things."

"No," Mrs. Mitchell said, her tone serious. "He's on a regular Boeing."

"It doesn't matter," Andy said. He didn't care. "I just hope my mom's okay."

Mrs. Mitchell looked away from him, turned her back completely and when she spoke, her voice warbled. "Where's your dad, Jason? He should be here by now."

The lady behind the ticket counter held up a large, round orange sticker. "Put this on your shirt where it can be seen easily."

"What's it for?" Andy asked, feeling small.

"Airport personnel waiting in Newport News will recognize you by that sticker and stay with you until an authorized person picks you up."

So it was for little kids, minors. He felt like a total tool for having to wear the stupid thing. They didn't care that he was scared to death about his mom. He had become just another headache, a passenger with a special need. Just a number on a piece of paper they called a boarding pass.

"We should head toward the gate." Mrs. Mitchell led him toward a line of passengers waiting to go through security.

"Wait," Mr. Mitchell called, his jowly face flushed as he jogged from the entrance to where they stood in line. "Everything go okay? Get your ticket?"

Mrs. Mitchell nodded and handed the ticket to Andy, holding onto his hand for a moment. "We'll see you soon. We're driving back right away and should be home by tomorrow afternoon."

Instead of letting go, she dragged him to her and hugged him like she would never see him again. It was awkward and weird.

Jason said, "Okay mom, let him go before the plane leaves without him."

Mr. Mitchell shook his hand. "You be careful, Andy. We'll see you soon."

Jason waved. "Hope your mom's okay, dude."

"Me too," Andy said and waved then hurried so he wouldn't hold up the line. On the other side of airport security, his backpack slung over his shoulder, he followed the signs to his boarding terminal. The thing seemed like it was on the other end of the earth. Every time he thought it would be down the next walkway, he had another to go. When he reached the right place, nearly all the passengers had already boarded.

He never saw the airplane from the outside. A long hallway attached the plane to the terminal where a flight attendant asked to see his boarding pass. Very friendly, she wore dark stockings and high heel shoes, the smell of fine perfume filled the air surrounding her. Inside the narrow passage to the seats, a gazillion buttons and compartments covered every surface.

Many of the seats were occupied. Andy looked at the numbers displayed on the overhead compartments. He tried to hold his backpack so no one would get hit in the head, but the aisle was very narrow and some of the passengers stared hard enough to make his face flush. He found his seat, the two beside it unoccupied.

Out the small window, the length of the wing didn't appear long enough to hold all the metal, steel, luggage, and passengers in the air. A high-pitched hum from the turbine engines signaled the start of the flight. He once was told that when a plane takes off, the power is so tremendous that you get pulled back into the seat.

Worry ate at the periphery of his mind and he carefully studied the interior, but it didn't help. He was surrounded by strangers, unsure of what to expect when he got home. Hopefully, his mom would be there, sitting at the kitchen table, arm in a sling and totally surprised to see him.

But why fly him home then? Why not call him? Who was paying for all this anyway?

What if she's not expected to live through the night?

Overhead, the speakers came to life as the attendants demonstrated the safety protocols in case of an emergency. Andy put the seat belt on and got a magazine from the pocket on the back of the seat in front of him. The plane eased slowly backward and he shoved the magazine back, gripping his armrests.

A lady up the aisle read a newspaper, her seat companion a magazine. They must have flown a million times to look so bored. A girl directly across from him stared out the window. She didn't look worried about take-off, even as the rpm's increased and the plane moved forward.

Over the speakers, came a tinny voice. "Welcome onboard flight two-seventy-four, nonstop to Newport News Virginia. Our travel time is approximately two hours and thirty minutes. We will be flying at an altitude of thirty thousand feet and will land at five-twenty-two p.m. We're second in line for takeoff and we'll be on our way here shortly."

What if the plane crashed? People don't survive plane crashes. If his mom had died, though, his own death would almost be a blessing. Maybe Fate wanted him to crash and die. His scalp prickled and he concentrated on trying to look like everyone else, blend in and not seem liked a freaked out kid who needed an orange sticker on his shirt.

The turbine engines increased to an alarming speed. As the brakes let go, the craft gained fascinating momentum, the overhead compartments rumbled. His hands locked tight around the armrests. Faster and faster the airplane accelerated. He closed his eyes.

I'm gonna die.

Eyes closed, the motion was worse, sickening him. He blinked and glanced out the window. The wing swayed slightly up and he hoped that was normal. Then the whole plane lifted and he didn't so much press back into his seat as his stomach dropped, like in an elevator. The rumble disappeared as they left the tarmac and only air rushed beneath them.

The girl across the aisle leaned back in her seat. She smiled calmly at him. Around his age, Andy thought.

The aircraft climbed higher and higher then leaned to one side suddenly and his heart lodged in his throat again. They leveled out and he understood they'd only adjusted course. He exhaled softly, praying he didn't make a fool of himself in front of all these strangers.

The smiling girl asked him, "Are you alright?"

His face burned and he offered a weak grin in return. "It's my first time flying."

"It's like taking a bus," she said. "Or a train only more boring because there's not as much to see."

Her composure worked its magic on him and he relaxed. Obviously she traveled a lot, so she knew what she was doing. He decided that if she spazzed out, then he would too, but until then, he would just enjoy the flight.

She actually talked to me.

He turned to the window to hide his smile. The patchwork world beneath them grew ever smaller as they continued to climb. Soon, clouds obscured the view and he understood what she meant about there not being much to see. As he turned away, sunlight broke through a cloudbank, filling the cabin with bright light. People turned, admiring the spectacle.

The shafts of golden light felt like a sign from above, maybe from his own father, that everything would be all right. His mom was okay. Her accident not nearly as bad as everyone made it out to be. Wouldn't the Mitchell's be relieved to know she was okay? They'd flip.

Overcome with joy, excited about being on a real airplane, it was as if he was on top of the world. His mom would be proud of him and he couldn't wait to tell Jason. He imagined his friend's big eyes and dropped jaw. He'd be totally jealous when Andy described the girl across the aisle. Maybe this was his paradise. Instead of a yacht, he would fly all around the world.

About halfway through the flight, attendants pushed carts down the aisles and gave out snacks and drinks. Just in time, he thought as his tummy growled. He folded the tabletop down.

She gave him a pleasant smile. "Something to drink? Pretzels?"

"Both please."

"And what would you like to drink, sir?"

Sir, she just called me sir?

"Orange juice, please." He took the pretzels. "Oh by the way, that uniform looks nice on you."

"Oh, thank you," she said, surprised as she filled a small cup with his juice. "Not often I meet a real gentleman."

The turbulent flight felt no different from the ride to school on a bus. He imagined the girl across the aisle handing him a piece of paper with her phone number and '*Call Me'* written on it, signed *Melissa*.

When he got home, he would call her. The daydream derailed, as he opened a door to find a funeral in progress instead of his living room. He drank his juice, gulping it down to get the lump out of his throat.

Did I tell her much I love her before I left?

A cold shiver went down his spine and he tried to think of nothing at all for the rest of the flight.

The plane dipped to a lower altitude. The captain's mellow voice filled the cabin. "Ladies and Gentlemen, we have started our descent and we'll be landing at Patrick Henry airport shortly. Current temperature is a sunny 78 degrees."

As he watched Newport News turn from a grid of farmland to neat rows of houses, he realized he had no clue who was gonna meet him. He could think of only two possibilities, either his Aunt Lily from Baltimore or Gary. He didn't know which one was worse. Probably Gary.

What if no one showed up at all?

The sticker on his shirt would keep him from finding his own way out of the airport and home. The airline didn't want to be sued for losing track of a minor, he figured. He had to get home, find his mother, not have some security guard baby-sit him out of pity. He peeled the sticker off and stuck it in the magazine bag below the tabletop. Hopefully, the flight crew wouldn't notice.

They flew low enough to see the nearby interstate. Buildings and vehicles appeared below. From the window Andy hunted for his neighborhood, but the quick descent didn't give him time to find any landmarks to help.

With the touchdown the rumble returned. A small price to pay to be safely back on the ground, he thought. The aircraft taxied slowly toward the airport terminal. In the distance the Patrick Henry sign stood tall. Only two days away, yet it felt as if he had been gone for years. Nothing looked the same, the colors cold and gray, so different from the breezy summer morning they packed the station wagon. His hometown appeared drained of life. He wished he'd never left in the first place. Maybe it wouldn't have changed at all.

Cleared to take off seat belts and exit the plane, he unbuckled, grabbed his bag, and stood up. Passengers blocked the aisle as they retrieved their belongings from the overhead compartments. He sat back down and waited patiently, not so eager to disembark. The girl across from him struggled to retrieve her bag. Too short, she couldn't get a good grip. He stood to help, freed the bag, and handed it to her.

This close, he noticed the green flecks in her eyes as she smiled. "Thank you."

He nodded, afraid to say something stupid. She smelled great, he thought as he stepped in the aisle, following her. A flight attendant stood by the door and wished everyone a good day. Most of the passengers ignored her as they walked by.

"Thank you," Andy said, feeling bad for her.

Shoulder to shoulder with his co-passengers, he felt part of the group. They just shared a special experience, flying on the same plane together. All these faces, total strangers, yet in a way all on the same team. Together, they shared the same fate.

They entered the building and the people he knew so briefly, spread out and disappeared. Nobody offered a friendly gesture or smiled at another passenger from the flight, even the girl from the opposite row walked by without one look in his direction. He shrank inside, feeling small, unimportant.

On my own again.

A man with a military haircut embraced a woman and two kids, the joy on their faces cutting through Andy, deepening his sorrow. Everyone from his flight disappeared, or met friends and loved ones. He recognized no one and no one came up to him. The girl who once smiled at him leapt into the waiting arms of a young guy holding flowers. She didn't care who was on the plane with her. Their kindness had all been fake. Nobody cared anymore.

He searched every woman of similar hair color, height, and build for his mom. None were even close.

He found the luggage carousel for his flight and waited there. Most likely anyone trying to find him would check there, right? His bag came down third, but he left it spinning on the platform as he studied anyone who wasn't carrying luggage—and might be looking for someone.

A few security guys and a girl in a white blouse and navy suit, like the attendants wore on the plane, stood talking by a water fountain. An old man, smelling of sweat and booze, sat on a bench by a bank of phones. The man slept, holding a newspaper with a hand missing two fingers. Thick scars gnarled the nubs where the digits had been and Andy turned away.

Still, no one came for him. Not Gary, not his mom, not even Aunt Lily. He recovered his bag and stood, dumb and alone, by the doors.

The bum on the bench probably had someone to meet him. Maybe someone from another plane. Or was he alone too? Is that how he'd turn out? Sleeping on a bench all alone in the airport, still waiting for someone to show up?

No one is coming because my mom is dead!

He gulped, throat so thick it hurt. No. No. Not that. He didn't want to cry, not in front of everyone. He rushed to the men's room. Safely inside a stall, the door locked, he sobbed.

Why is this happening?

He punched the metal wall, hurting his knuckles. "Why!"

If God existed, he wanted to know why he was being punished so much. Was he like some axe murderer in another life? What had he done?

When he couldn't cry anymore, he dried his eyes and left the stall. The only thing he could think to do was go home. He didn't have any real money at all. Just a few bucks in his pocket. Enough to get home on a bus, if he was careful.

Dragging his feet and lugging his bags, he navigated the bus system and got as close to home as he could. He walked the last six blocks or so until he could cut across his lawn. No lights shone; no cars in the driveway. The whole place was dark. He plodded up the front porch, hoping he'd find his mom in a neck brace, sleeping on the couch or something—anything where she was actually alive.

It's all just a bad dream. Let it all be a bad dream, please?

He used the spare key and opened the door. "Mom?"

Nothing.

"Mom?" His voice echoed. Why didn't anyone answer his desperate shouts?

He sobbed, giving in, letting go, howling in pain and rage. He knocked down chairs, swept the sideboard in the hall clean. A porcelain vase shattered into a thousand pieces on the hardwood floor. He raced upstairs, to his bedroom. Breathing heavily, his eyes fell instantly on the framed picture on the nightstand. He lunged for the frame, ripped the photograph free, and brushed the image with one, trembling finger.

He wiped the tears from his eyes with his sleeve and folded the picture into his back pocket then took off running down the staircase. At the front door, the phone suddenly rang. He stopped, mouth wide, gasping for air, staring at the ringing phone in the kitchen. What if it was his mom calling the house looking for him?

He slowly approached the half open door. Knees shaking, he pushed the door wide, eyes glued to the phone, mind racing, sweat running down his collar. He debated whether he should answer or let the old machine pick up. While he stood there, frozen, the call went to the machine.

"Where's my nephew? This is his Aunt Lily, you can reach me at ..." She gave her number, sounding angry. "Is someone gonna tell me when Nancy's funeral is? Or do I get to hear about it after the fact. Someone better call me."

Mom is dead.

No!

"No!" He picked up the phone, drew back, and slammed it against the wall. Shattered remains tumbled to the floor. An earpiece tangled by two wires screeched a dial tone. He stared furiously at the broken pieces.

No! It's not true!

"It's not true," he whispered, choking on the words. "Oh God, it can't be true."

The dial tone ended and a recording began, *"If you'd like to make a call, please hang up and dial again."*

He kicked the phone's remains across the room.

Think! Think!
Mom is dead.

He released a throaty scream, head back, hands grasping his hair as he spun in a circle, not knowing where to go. Across the darkened dining room, he spotted a bottle of extra special whiskey in the china cabinet. Before he could think, he rushed to open the glass door and pulled the bottle from the shelf.

He unscrewed the top and chugged. It burned, ran down his face, into the collar of his shirt. The taste was horrible and he dropped the bottle, letting it clunk on the carpet and spill. He stared, eyes blurred by fresh tears. His mom would never ground him for this, never scold him, or ask him what had gotten into him.

Never again.

Because she's dead like Dad! Dead! Both of them!

He couldn't stay there. Couldn't look around and see his mom's favorite painting above the couch, see his dad's favorite chair in the corner. They were gone now, never coming back.

Never coming back.

He ran out of the house, slamming the door shut behind him. Aimlessly he ran, as fast as he could, never able to escape the blackness slithering into his mind, charring what remained of who he was.

CHAPTER 10

Carry on Wayward Son

Frank button-hooked the big semi into the empty lot of an abandoned store a few blocks from Andy's house. The air brakes hissed and the engine died with a rattle he felt beneath his seat. Two days on the road, and he still got caught off guard.

"That's it kiddo, finally back in good old Newport Snooze." He adjusted the cap on his head and began shutting down the interior of the truck. "The wife will be here soon. She can give you a lift to your place, if you want?"

"Naw, I'll just walk. Want to stretch my legs anyway. I had fun. Thanks for taking me," Andy gibbered then smiled, pretending he wasn't triple scared he'd be caught in his lies. "We gotta do that again someday."

"Anytime kiddo, anytime." Frank smoothed down his whiskers, his mustache so thick a bird could lay an egg in the mass. "I keep my promises. Next time, don't take five years to let me make good on it though, 'kay?"

"It's a deal." He shouldered his backpack and grasped the moist handle, opening the door and stepping down. "Well I guess I'll see you around."

"You betcha," Frank said, "And, hey…"

He held the door open and his breath. *Here it comes. He's gonna say he knew all along I was lying.*

"Tell your ma I said not to be a stranger. She can call if she needs anything."

"Will do, sir." Andy smiled and shut the truck door, landing on the cracked pavement and exhaling hugely.

Dad....

He started to walk, sure Frank still watched him. The trip had been great. Seeing Knoxville and going through the Smoky Mountain range would have been very cool if it didn't hurt so much that he wasn't seeing all that with his own dad. At least Frank was happy to take him out, believing Andy's story that he was bored while his mom was camping in Greensboro and she couldn't be reached.

He missed his dad more than ever now. Riding in the semi, needing him like he never had before, there was only one place he wanted to go.

Though not hot like during the day, the night air was still muggy. Glowing mist surrounded every streetlight, reminding him of the clouds beneath the plane on his way back from Syracuse. As the street took him out of sight, he relaxed more, walking right on past the road to his house. He wouldn't go back there. Not now anyway. Bad things were back there and he had scrubbed it all from his mind, dissolving the memories with the battery acid of the pain they caused.

Images boiled up, wanting to break the surface of his thoughts, but he shoved them back down easily, having gotten good at it over the last two days on the road with Frank. He straightened his back—just a guy out for a stroll. A normal guy with a normal life. By the time he entered Warwick Boulevard, he only thought of the sound of his shoes, the weight of his pack, the way the trees glistened.

Andy crossed near Culver as the thick clouds passed over the moon, compressed the air. Just a few more yards and he would reach the woods and the worn path of pine needles and dead leaves that would take him directly to Main Street.

He and his Dad used to cut through there all the time on their bikes. Walking took longer, but not long enough. The shadows should have frightened him, but they didn't. He welcomed them, hid within them, becoming a shadow himself and all too soon, he left the path behind and started up the gravel road to the cemetery.

His sneaker hit grass and he started counting, like he had every time he'd come since he was a kid. Eighty even, just as he remembered. Eighty steps to his father. He sent a silent apology for not visiting in so long as he knelt and wove his fingers through the grass, pressing his palm into the moist earth where he imagined his dad's shoulder might be. "Hey, dad."

Soft drops of rain, warm at first, cooled his heated skin, felt nice. Face turned to the sky, he opened his mouth, eyes closed. The slightly mineral clean taste spread across his tongue, wet his throat. The gentle patter turned to a downpour, soaking him through, the ground going soggy beneath his knees. But it didn't matter. Nothing mattered.

Wash it away...just wash it all away.

I'll be back, Andy thought, and wiped water from the gravestone. He sank in the thick grass and when he reached the gravel road his sneakers were full of water. Everything in his pack would get wet too, he knew, but he just tucked his chin down and kept moving. He wondered what life would be like if he just turned into the woods, built him a hut or something, and lived there by himself for the rest of his life, like a hermit.

There was a whole wide world out there though and he had gotten a taste for the road now. All the places he hadn't seen. All the places that weren't here, weren't where he had lived happily once. In a town where...

He shut those thoughts out, concentrating on the downgrade of the road to keep from slipping on the loose gravel. Yeah, better just to get away, get out of town. Memories were easier to ignore when there weren't so many reminders.

He climbed the guardrail and started down the parkway, hands tucked in his pockets head bowed so the rain ran in thick rivulets from his bangs. Cars went by, some splashing him as they got too close, though he kept as far away as he could.

One step in front of the other...

A brown van sped by then slowed, easing onto the shoulder and stopping ahead. The reverse lights came on and he stopped walking to watch. The rusted van braked five feet from him. An arm stuck out the passenger side window and waved him forward.

High stepping over tall weeds and trying not to drag himself along the van, he eased along the guardrail to the window.

A girl, her makeup bright, eyelids sparkling smiled. "You alright? You lost?"

What could he say? He wasn't all right, but he wasn't

106

going to tell her what was wrong because that meant remembering and he wasn't going to do that. He couldn't tell her he was lost because he knew exactly where he was. He just didn't know where to go.

"Are you in some kind of trouble?"

Before he could reply, the side door slid open and a guy charged out, unzipping his pants.

Startled Andy backed up.

"Ahh," the guy said, his long blond hair turning dark with rain. "Sorry man. I had to piss bad."

"Ignore him," the girl said, laughing. "You want a ride? Better than walking in the rain, right?"

Her laughter convinced him and he smiled. "Right."

"Well, get in then, I'm getting soaked." Still smiling, she rolled her window up.

He meant to follow the blonde back into the van, but the guy tripped over his own feet and fell, slamming his ribs hard on the running board.

Twisted in her seat, she said, "Oh my God, Brandon, are you okay?"

Without thinking, Andy held his hand out to help the guy up.

"Yeah, just peachy," Brandon said as he stood and uttered a thanks to Andy before climbing all the way in.

"Did you get hurt?" she asked as Andy bent in after him.

Brandon said, "No, it tickled. Yeah I got hurt, scraped my side up, but I'm cool. No need to start crying for me."

She grinned and threw a balled up burger wrapper at him. "Shut up."

"Well, don't just stand there," Brandon said to Andy.

"Sit down and close the door."

"I'm all wet," he said, afraid to soak their upholstery.

"These seats seen a lot worse than a little rain water, dude."

"Okay." He sat on the edge of the seat closest to the sliding door and slammed it shut. As soon as it closed, the van started moving again, merging into traffic.

"I'm Sarah." She held out a hand and as he shook it, she said, "And if you haven't figured it out yet, that's Brandon; don't mind him he is an idiot."

"I'm Andy."

"This is Kevin," she said, gesturing to the driver. Probably twenty something and broad across the shoulders.

He raised a hand. "Hey," he said, but he didn't look back.

Andy said, "Hey."

"Jilly," Sarah shouted. "Jilly, wake up, we got company."

He turned as a girl's face appeared above the back of his seat. Freckles across her nose, curly red hair pulled up in a ponytail on top of her head, she blinked at him. "Who are you?"

"He's Andy," Sarah said before he could answer. "We're giving him a lift."

"Okay," she said, smiling. "Hi, Andy."

"Hi."

She disappeared out of sight again and Sarah said, "Don't mind her. She worked all day and wants to get some sleep in so she can stay up all night."

"Where were you going?" Brandon asked.

Andy shrugged. "Just to see a friend."

"We can drop you off," Sarah said. "Or at least get close. We're on our way to Virginia Beach to see Nickelback. If it's along the way, it's no problem."

"My friend lives in Virginia Beach," Andy said quickly. "I'll just ride there with you, if that's okay?"

"And you were just gonna *walk* there?" Bandon asked.

Andy's face blazed. "Well, no. I was hoping I'd talk my uncle into giving me a ride. But he's a real jerk and probably wouldn't."

"Well, guess it's your lucky night then." Sarah eyed him as the radio played a heavy rock song Andy didn't know. "I think you're a little smaller than my brother, but you should be able to fit into his jersey. At least you can get out of those wet things."

"I'm okay," he said, though the wet clothes clung to him and in the air-conditioning, he shivered.

"Yeah, right," Sarah said, her smile softening the sarcasm. "Brandon, look under that seat. My bag should be there. Pull out the white jersey for him."

Brandon bent and felt along beneath where he was sitting and came up empty. "Nothing there."

"Here," Sarah said, "trade places with me."

They exchanged seats, but instead of Sarah sitting down, she kneeled and leaned over the back. Andy didn't look at the tattoo above the line of her jeans. He didn't look at it at all.

"Got it," she announced and sat down, holding the white shirt triumphantly. "It's my brother, Darryl's old jersey. I use it as a nightgown, but it should fit you okay. Try it on."

Like right there? In front of all of them? "I'm really okay. I'm not even wet anymore."

Sarah handed him the jersey and smiled sweetly, "Take it, go on."

"Okay okay." Andy gave in.

Crap.

Scrawny didn't even begin to describe his hairless, caved in chest and thin arms. Compared to the driver, he was a Slim Jim.

Worse, Sarah scooted closer to help him roll the wet shirt clinging to his soaked skin.

"I got it." Andy tugged and pulled, in a hurry to switch out before she could really notice him in the dark.

"Don't be a baby. You're twisted." Sarah yanked the shirt over his head, making his hair stand up. He liked the attention, but not when he wasn't wearing a shirt. He slipped into the dry jersey much faster than he'd gotten out of the wet shirt. Number twenty-four, he thought, straightening the sleeves out and already warming up.

"Careful, kid. She bites," Kevin called.

"Shut up or I'm gonna bite you." She laughed.

"Promise?" He cocked a grin.

"Watch the road." Sarah sat back and waved her hand. "Don't mind them."

He played with the sleeve of the jersey, wishing he could just chill, be cool like the guy who played Hit Man and not some dork. *Korn* came on the radio and Brandon turned up the volume. The guys in the front rocked it out, nodding to the beat.

"Feel better?" She asked low enough they wouldn't hear

her above the music.

"Yeah," he said, afraid to look at her.

She was cool though and didn't bomb him with a ton of questions or talk just for the sake of talking, unlike just about every girl he'd ever met. She was so laid back; he relaxed around her and imagined what it might be like to just live in the van with them, going from concert to concert, beach to beach. That would be cool.

His mood plummeted as Scars on Broadway blasted through the speakers; the irony of *Universe* playing at that moment laid all his carefully created normalcy to waste. He wouldn't cry in front of Sarah like the big baby she already thought he was. Every lyric asking a mother about dying twisted in his chest, calling up memories that shouldn't exist anymore.

He closed his eyes, wishing he was in the car with his mom instead of all these strangers. Her slender hands rested, beautiful and tender, one on the shifter the other on the wheel. Sunlight dappled across her face as they passed beneath the arch of trees above the road. He heard her voice again, always saying the same thing.

You must be strong now, Andy.

Her smile turned to a scream as a truck smashed into her, crumpling the car as if it was made from paper. Glass shattered, spraying her face, cutting into her flesh.

Andy jerked and opened his eyes.

Go away.

Go away.

Nothing happened.

Nothing happened at all.

"Wow," Sarah said beside him. "What were you thinking? I've never seen anyone turn that white in my life."

"Nothing," he mumbled.

She studied him for a minute then said, "Would you like some water?"

He shook his head and turned away, watching speed limit and ramp signs pass.

Her hand, warm on his shoulder, surprised him, but he didn't look at her, too afraid she'd see he was near tears.

"Whatever it was," she said, "I'm sure you'll be okay."

He wasn't so sure.

Kevin got off the interstate, coming to a stop at the bottom of the off ramp. "Ya'll got your tickets right?"

Tickets?

He had maybe fifteen bucks left from what Frank gave him for helping untarp his load in Knoxville, but no tickets. His only food money—he couldn't afford a ticket. "I'll just go hang out with my friend."

"What friend?" Sarah asked, raising her brows.

"The one that lives here," he said quickly.

"What's his name?"

"Jason."

"Where does he live?"

"Not far from the beach."

"Good, we'll drop you off. Just give Kevin directions."

"Uh," Andy said. "I can walk. It's okay. It even stopped raining."

"No can do. We picked you up, now we're gonna make sure you're safe. Besides, what if your friend isn't home?"

He didn't answer. Here were the gazillion questions he

112

didn't want to answer.

Lower she said, "There's no friend, is there Andy?"

He slumped, unable to look in her face. "No."

She grinned and squeezed his knee briefly. "That settles it then, you're coming with us."

"I don't have enough money. I got..." He dug in his jeans and held up the crumpled bills. "Thirteen dollars and some change. That's not enough is it?"

"Kevin?" Sarah asked.

The driver sighed. "I got five."

"Brandon?"

"I can pitch in about ten. But that's it."

"I've got a few bucks too," she said. "Should be enough to get you a ticket from a scalper. No biggie."

"Not so sure," Jilly said from the backseat as she sat up. "Getting in to see Nickleback ain't gonna be easy. I got our tickets like a month ago and it was tough then."

"Oh c'mon, Jilly," Sarah pleaded. "You know *everyone*. At least try. I swear on my brother's life I'll pay you back."

Jilly exhaled like a deflating balloon and frowned. "Yeah it's a miracle Darryl's still a free man as many times you put him up as collateral."

Kevin laughed as Jilly pulled her cell phone out.

Sarah grinned. "You know you love me."

She just rolled her eyes and sat back. "Hey, Jack, I gotta question for you..."

The streets grew congested as they neared the amphitheater. Brandon muttered, "Should call this bottle neck road."

Bumper to bumper, they waited their turn to get onto the

grounds. Jillian closed her phone. "He's gotta call me back."

"Thanks," Andy said. Total strangers were being so cool to him. He didn't know why, but he thought maybe it was his dad looking out for him again.

"Jeez, it's backed up all the way to here already," Kevin said, pulling into the first empty slot the traffic directors sent him toward. "We're gonna have to hike it the rest of the way."

Everywhere people exited their cars and trucks, creating a large, shifting crowd moving in the general direction of the concert. The guys walked ahead, leaving Jilly and Sarah behind with Andy. He didn't mind. He preferred to stay close to Sarah.

Halfway there, Jilly's phone rang. "Yep," she said. "Oh man. That sucks. Yeah, okay."

Sarah asked, "Not good?"

She shook her head. "Sorry, kid. They've been sold out for two weeks. If we had like five hundred bucks, then maybe…"

Sarah sighed. "Well we can't just leave him."

"That's okay," Andy said. He wasn't some kid that needed babysitting. "I can take care of myself."

She raised an eyebrow. "That's why you were walking in the rain with nowhere to go?"

He blushed.

"Leave him be, Sarah," Jilly said. "We're gonna miss everything if we stand around here talking all night. Take care, kid." She waved at him and rushed to catch up with Brandon and Kevin.

"You sure you're gonna be okay?" Sarah asked,

114

glancing back to her friends.

"Yeah," he said, throwing his backpack over one shoulder. "Thanks for the lift."

To his surprise, she gave him a quick hug. "Be careful out there, Andy. And keep the shirt. Maybe it'll bring you luck."

"Thanks," he said, imagining what she might do if he kissed her. Probably slap him in the face. Instead, he waved a little and watched her walk away.

Alone again, he decided to let his stomach lead the way. They'd passed a sub place back on the road and he could walk there, get something to eat, and figure out what to do next. Moving through the crowd proved tough as everyone else headed in the opposite direction. He wondered what it would be like when the concert was over. Probably twice as bad getting out as getting in. Even so, he wished he could have stayed with Sarah longer.

The walk took forever and by the time he got to the sub shop, his legs ached. He stood behind an older man wearing shorts and black socks. Even if he lived to be a thousand, he'd never wear something like that.

"Hey are you in line?" A kid his age with long hair and cowboy boots asked.

"Yeah," Andy said, then turned back to study the menu board. He wanted something hot.

The guy behind him stood uncomfortably close and he swore he felt breath on his neck.

"So you like hockey?" the kid asked, his breath hot on Andy's ear.

"What?"

"Your jersey." He nodded to Andy's shirt.

Andy mumbled, "Just something someone gave me."

"Yeah I can tell it doesn't fit you too well."

Of course the old guy ahead of him had to pay in exact change. He took forever, counting out nickels and pennies. Andy urged him to hurry so he could get away from the guy behind him.

"Hey, you got a buck you can spare?" the grimy teen asked. "Dude, I'm starving and I just realized I forgot my wallet back at home. Got a cash flow problem. I'll pay you back, honest."

Andy thought of saying no, but when he looked in the kid's eyes, he pictured the guy waiting for him outside, a knife or even a gun in his hand. "Yeah, I got a dollar for you."

"Thanks, man," he said. "You're up. Mind if I just add my order to yours, in case there's tax or something?"

Andy shook his head. Maybe he was supposed to help this guy out, the way Sarah had helped him. Maybe it was some kind of test or something. They ordered their food and he ended up spending four bucks on the guy.

"You're really a cool guy," he said as they picked a table. "You want to come back with me? Meet some of my friends? I can pay you back then."

He had nowhere else to go. "Sure, okay."

"Awesome." Mouth opened hugely, he bit off half his meatball sub, cheeks expanding around the wad of food, sauce smeared across one cheek. "Wait'll you see our place. It's out on the beach and it's totally free."

"Free?" Andy asked.

116

"Yep," he said, still chewing his first bite. "You'll have to spring for bus fare though. Unless you wanna walk—but it's like miles."

Andy saw the last of his money disappearing—but for a free place to spend the night? The cost of bus fare didn't seem that big of a deal. "Okay. Sounds good."

He had a new friend, a place to sleep for free and a future without memories.

Andy smiled.

PART III

Torn From Normal

CHAPTER 11

Virginia Beach Boys

All morning long Danny's dad Marvin had been acting strange. He kept checking his watch, sighing and wandering around. Two days of rain could to do that to a person, Danny thought, feeling a bit of cabin fever himself. But he wasn't so totally bored that when his dad wanted to clean the garage he jumped for joy.

"Let's just see how far we get, okay?" Marvin asked, his mind miles away as he stood in the center of the garage and stared at nothing.

Danny shrugged. From one of the shelves that lined half of the garage, he dragged a box full of junk. He pawed through the stuff and waited for his father to tell him what to do. He stood there waiting, then gave up and asked, "What's with you, Dad?"

He shook himself. "Don't know what's wrong. I keep thinking I forgot something or I'm supposed to be somewhere but I've double checked everything and there's nothing I'm missing."

Okay, his dad wasn't old enough to start going all Old-timers on him, was he? "I'm sure you'll remember. What do you want to do with this stuff?"

He glanced at the box. "Sort through it and throw anything away that doesn't work."

Great, this was going to be a real purge. Worse as they worked, the rain tapered off and sun peeked from between the remaining clouds. The humidity rose and his t-shirt grew damp and uncomfortable.

Forty-five minutes into their abysmal progress, Danny's father stopped, which was odd because they guy was compulsive about finishing anything he started. "What do you say we go for a spin? See where the road takes us and get out of this stuffy garage?"

Danny grinned, not at his father, but at the convertible Porsche in the driveway. "Now you're talkin'!"

Maybe his dad wasn't something awesomely cool like a rock star, but he had great taste in cars. The sour face he'd worn all morning morphed into that look a kid gets at Christmas when he sees what Santa left under the tree. Danny didn't feel one bit different. Secretly he had been working on a sales pitch that would get his father to give him the keys for his next birthday.

Dad, you really need new wheels. Everyone's seen you in this already. C'mon, Dad, you know you want that new model they came out with this year. I hear it totally blows your old one away. Besides, I'll need something more reliable than my station wagon to get back and forth to work.

He could hope, right?

Danny opened the door to the Porsche, sliding into the passenger seat as his father got behind the wheel. His dad started the engine and the CD came on automatically, the techno beat thumping in his chest.

Marvin engaged the clutch, put her in first, and backed

into the driveway. "The garage can wait, hey?"

"It ain't going nowhere."

"Not going anywhere," his father said, smiling. "It's not going anywhere."

Danny rolled his eyes, turned up the music, and let the wind blow in his hair, lifting it from his forehead. The sun shone, the air still smelled like rain, but the oppressive humidity vanished in the slipstream of the convertible hitting fifty.

At the onramp, the light turned red and a black two-door Civic pulled alongside him. The guy revved his engine and jerked his chin up, eyes hidden by oversized glasses. Danny laughed and turned to his dad, jerking a thumb at the driver. "Get a load of this tool."

When Marvin looked, the guy revved his engine again, smacking his gum.

"What do you say?" Danny urged, having never been able to get his father to let the car out while he was a passenger. The speeding tickets his dad got proved the man could really push her if he wanted. "Show 'em what you got, Dad."

The far green light turned yellow. Not much time to decide.

His dad looked back and forth again, this time the other driver waved him off, like he was too much of a wuss to accept the challenge.

Maybe it was the odd mood his dad had been in all morning, or maybe it was because Danny was about to turn eighteen, but whatever got into his father, he loved it. His dad slammed on the accelerator a fraction of a second before the light turned green and flew up the on ramp.

Gears low, rpm's high, the jerk beside them obviously didn't know that the Porsche had longer gears and more torque on the upper end. No way could his half souped-up piece of Japanese engineering keep up. Danny threw his head back and laughed as they accelerator climbed, the longer lengths of his hair prickling his temples as they whipped in the wind.

They stuck side by side for a moment, his father actually toying with the other driver to make him think he had a chance in hell of beating the Porsche. Then with an undeniable boost, he unleashed the power beneath the hood. Flattened into his seat, Danny held on, grinning wide and praying a bug didn't hit his teeth. The open road flashed by, the other driver left to eat their dust.

His father slowed rather quickly, forcing him to strain against his seatbelt as they lost momentum. Danny laughed. "That was awesome. You blew that guy away."

"Well, don't tell anyone," his father admonished, but he was smiling. "What do you say I take you to my old stomping grounds?"

As many times as his dad had taken him to Virginia Beach to visit his *old stomping grounds* never did he sound like he remembered the five million previous times they'd gone. That was okay though, Danny didn't mind. "Can we stop at that flea market thing we went to last time?"

He nodded and they fell into a comfortable silence. The radio played the wind smelled fresh and the Porsche ran at a fine-tuned hum. The scent of the ocean grew stronger, a gull appearing overhead now and again, its white fat belly backlit by a high sun. They took an exit and chose the boulevard running parallel to the interstate.

"Guess George at the Caddy dealership is running a summer special," his father muttered as they passed a huge lot with bright signs and balloons advertising the sale.

His dad always wanted to know what the competition was up to. Danny wondered if he'd ever get one of those corporate spy types to dig up dirt on major dealerships in the surrounding five counties.

The traffic slowed, turning into bumper-to-bumper traffic, yet instead of getting irate, his dad sat up straighter, the energy pouring off the guy quadrupling. Though it wasn't his car, he sat a little straighter as he scoped out the other makes and models trapped with them on the boulevard.

"I ever tell you," his father said as the CD ended. "I can't pass the 'Welcome to Virginia Beach' sign without getting all sentimental? Eighteen years ago your old man came to the United States. I started my new life here. On the other side of that ocean is my homeland, but I don't look back. This is where dreams come true."

Danny nodded absently, wondering what it felt like to be a brand new immigrant, full of all kinds of crazy ideas about America. Most of the dudes he knew back then were all gone. A lot of them, he guessed they were in the military now. Weird how just living somewhere different can change your whole life.

They drew stares of envy, the Porsche working its magic on the beach crowd. A group of guys stood off to the side getting ready to dodge traffic and cross the boulevard. Homeless kids, probably, from the scraggly way they looked and the floppy, multi-colored hair. Last year Joey Strongs, a junior, had run away from home and ended up down on the beach. When they caught him and brought him back, he told stories about all the creepy people late at night around there.

His dad turned off the boulevard and headed to their favorite little flea market. They parked and put the top up, locking the doors. Not the worst area, but not good enough to leave the car open and unlocked.

Mini-vans, pick-up trucks, and station wagons brought people to exchange junk for cash. Danny split from his dad and went to hunt through CD's that looked like they'd been out within the last decade while his father flipped through music as old as dirt. Nothing good, just a bunch of one hit wonders that weren't that great to begin with.

His cell phone rang; the display name was Ryan, a kid his dad fostered when Danny was barely out of kindergarten. "Hey buddy, what's up?"

"I'm in town. Thought we might get together and knock down some pins."

"Cool. I'm sure Dad will be up for it. He barely knows what to do with himself, all fidgety and stuff. How's the new job?"

"Working me like a dog." A smile warmed his voice. "I'm pulling extra shifts to save up for next semester. You still slaving away?"

"Yeah, full time now that school's out." A horn honked loudly beside him and he nearly dropped the phone. "Jeez."

"Where are you?" When he told him, Ryan asked, "What are you doing there?"

"Cleaning the garage sucked, especially with all this

126

humidity. Dad wanted to take the Porsche out and we ended up here."

"Lazy bums, the both of you."

Danny grinned. "Yeah, yeah. How does the alley in Newport News sound?"

"About nine-thirty?"

"Okay. If Dad freaks, I'll call and tell you, but I'm pretty sure he'd get a kick out of seeing you again."

"Cool."

They hung up and Danny surveyed the long tables laden with unwanted possessions, hunting for his father. The guy liked to get in quick and out quicker when it came to flea markets. Hit and run, he liked to say, drive-by shopping. Or they'd end up with a car full of useless junk, even if it was sort of cool.

His dad was sorting through a stack of CD's a booth over, but behind him, a tall skinny guy waved his arms, voice rising above the chatter of shoppers. He pointed and Danny followed the line of his finger. Those kids he'd seen jaywalking milled near a booth filled with baggy gangsta jeans and cheap looking Orange County Chopper knock-off T-shirts. Danny maneuvered between the stalls, heading for his father.

"They're no good. Kids get busted here at least once a week for stealing. They should put an age limit on who can come here without an adult." The tall guy put his hands on his hips, face flushed.

"What's going on?" Danny asked his dad.

He shrugged. "I don't know. They don't look like they're doing anything wrong. Hey, he's wearing my lucky number."

127

A kid in a too-big, number twenty-four white hockey jersey stared grimly at another kid in leather and cowboy boots. Grimy hair and a ripped t-shirt only made him look more like a loser. Who wore boots to the beach?

"They're not allowed to skateboard in here. Look, that punk's got one under his arm." The tall man directed his shouted reminder of the rules toward the kids and the one in leather looked up and scowled. The brown-haired guy with the skateboard said something that made them all laugh.

"C'mon, there's one more table I want to check before we leave." His father steered him through the crowd, aiming for a far stall beyond the boys. As they went, Danny told him about the phone call from Ryan and their plans to go bowling later on. "Sure, sounds good. Guess you didn't really want to finish that garage today."

Danny returned his father's grin and said, "Oh come on, you were the one who said we should give up and go for a drive."

"Got me there."

They flipped through the CD's lined up in low wooden crates, filling the entire stall. Lots of people squeezed in around them, all hunting for some obscure title. Danny didn't really care about it all that much, though he got a few chuckles out of some of the sillier names like Ultimate Spinach. Who in the heck thought that sounded good?

"Found it," his father said triumphantly. He held up a CD that read, *A-ha: Analogue.* "Must have been seeing my lucky number. I've been wanting this for years."

"I can tell. Must have come out before the dinosaurs." Danny grinned.

"Funny, funny. You just wait," he said, paying the vendor. "One of these days the stuff you like today will be elevator music for your kids."

"Doubt it." Danny tried to imagine *Rammstein* bounced out on a xylophone or some other lame-o instrument.

"You'll see," he said, following Danny back through the crowd. "I didn't think it was possible either."

The customers were thick as they hit the busiest time of day. His father took over, leading them toward the car. Before he reached it though, that tall guy tapped him on the shoulder, practically elbowing Danny in the head to reach him. "Yes?"

"Those kids over there." He breathed heavy, as if he'd run to tell Danny's father something about the kids he appeared to hate. "I saw the one with the long hair. He took your wallet."

Marvin felt for the wallet and then turned to look at him with surprise. "He's right. My wallet's gone. I could have left it back there when I bought the CD."

"I saw you put it back in your pocket, Dad. I was right there." Oh jeez, just what he needed—creepy teens giving everyone a bad impression of guys his age. He hated jerks like that.

The tall guy yelled, "Someone stop those kids! They stole this guy's wallet!"

Grimy hair threw something at the kid in the white jersey and shouted. "Run!"

The kid stood there for a moment, looking confused, but when the tall man started after him, followed by Marvin, and then Danny who didn't want to miss anything, he turned tail and ran with the rest of his friends.

Everyone stood paralyzed; no one moved to stop the kids from getting away. Amazed, Danny tucked that info away for future use. Note to self: crowds are stupid creatures that move slowly. Even when they were slapping pavement, the older men ahead actually doing a pretty good job of keeping up, people wandered into their path like zombies in a shopping daze. Then they'd snap too and jerk away, gasping as if they had appeared out of nowhere.

Despite the people in their path, the street kids were fast. The two teens out front jumped over displays of toys and garden equipment, then split in two directions. The kid in leather could really book it and the tall man took after him, maybe guessing Danny's dad didn't have his long-legged speed.

The other one dropped his skateboard, hopped on and there was no hope of catching him. Danny started to get a stitch in his side and couldn't imagine how his father must have felt, being less in shape than he was. The guy had to be running on adrenalin or something. The kid in the white jersey glanced back, saw Marvin slowing down, and did the freakiest thing.

He stopped running.

Danny could hardly believe it as he slowed beside his father, who was bent at the waist and a few shades of alarming red. He panted and put a hand on Danny's elbow to straighten up.

The kid watched his dad warily, his glance barely flicking to Danny at all. Guess he feared the guy they'd robbed more than another guy his age.

"What's he waiting for?" Danny asked below his breath.

Even as he spoke, the kid took a few steps forward, then bent and carefully laid the wallet on the asphalt. He backed away, hands up and when Danny and his father stepped forward he said, "Sorry. I didn't know they took it."

Danny's dad recovered his wallet, checked inside and said. "It's all here." He put it securely deep in his pants pocket. "Thanks."

Saying thanks was totally not necessary, Danny thought. Even if the kid hadn't been in on stealing the wallet, he'd run with them. Still, he looked about as dangerous as Barney the purple dinosaur.

He nodded once and turned, jogging as if afraid Marvin would change his mind and try to catch him to press charges. Unfortunately, he should have worried about that tall guy coming back because he ran right into him.

They scuffled, the man yanking him by the arm and shaking him hard enough to make his head rattle back and forth. The tall man yelled, "Gotcha, you little punk!"

"Hey," Danny's father yelled. "Wait. Don't do that. He gave my wallet back. He gave it back. Stop."

The kid had tears in his eyes. "I didn't do anything. Let me go. Please. You're hurting my arm."

Danny was surprised by how young the guy sounded. He'd taken him to be closer to his age, but wondered if he wasn't just tall for his age.

"You robbed him!" The guy shouted into the kid's face as those heading into the flea market either gave them a wide berth, or stopped to stare. "I saw you! The cops are on the way. I called them already and you're not going anywhere until they get here."

"That's really not necessary," Marvin said, holding up his hands as he moved closer, the way he had once done to a runaway dog whose leash got stuck in their fence and he had to get close enough to free the pet.

"You gotta believe me." The boy turned pleading eyes on them both. "Tell him I gave it back. I didn't do anything."

Sirens sounded in the distance, growing closer.

Danny ventured, "He's telling the truth. I saw it. The guy in leather that you let get away was the one who had my dad's wallet."

"Danny," his father cautioned. "Let me handle this. Sir, my son is right. This is the wrong kid."

"He committed larceny!" His face turned purple. "I'll perform a citizen's arrest if I have to."

The kid howled as the man yanked his arm up behind his back, twisting the wrist cruelly.

"That is totally unnecessary. Remove your hands from that boy and let the police deal with him or I'll have you brought up on charges for assaulting a minor."

Go, Dad!

Years of fostering boys in their house had given his dad that edge of authority some other guy might not have had. The tall dude seemed to know it too because he slacked off and began stammering about gratitude. The squad car arrived and drowned out the rest of what he said.

His father looked relieved to see the police officers as they silenced the siren and exited their vehicle. They were big guys and even though Danny had never been in any trouble with the law, they made him remember all the stuff

132

he might get in trouble for—like not wearing his seatbelt or jaywalking or that time he spat his gum on the sidewalk. Did they have a law for that?

"What's going on here?" The first asked as the other spoke into the radio at his shoulder.

"I saw this punk," the tall man yelled, "steal that man's wallet."

He pointed at Danny's father who held up his hands. "I didn't see the wallet get taken, but there were two other kids. I think this one was just in the wrong place at the wrong time."

"Sir," the second officer said to long, tall and deranged. "Please take your hands off the boy. I'll need to search him."

"Sure thing, officer." The man let go, stepped back, and crossed his arms. He watched, gloating as the police officer led number twenty-four to a cruiser.

"You got any weapons on you? Any needles?" The officer patted the kid down.

The boy shook his head, face pale, disbelief in his eyes. While his partner approached the tall man, the officer placed his hand on the kid's head and forced him into the back seat. The door closed with a loud snick. Not like the movies at all, Danny thought. There was no thrill in seeing the crook captured. This boy looked more like a kicked puppy getting hauled away by the dogcatcher—absolutely pitiful.

"Dad," Danny said. "I saw the one in boots throw your wallet at this guy. I don't think he did anything wrong."

The tall man crowed, "I said those kids were up to no good. Maybe if *people*," he gave Marvin a pointed look, "would have listened to me, this wouldn't have happened.

We have to stand up and do what's right or we'll all have our wallets stolen."

The police officer who frisked the kid asked Marvin, "Your wallet was taken out of your pocket, is that correct?"

"Yes, but I don't think this boy robbed me. My son and I both saw another boy toss my wallet at him. He was confused, didn't even run away until he someone told him to."

Danny had forgotten about that part. Now he was even more convinced that this guy didn't deserve to take the rap for what the other one had done.

"Did you get your wallet back?" The cop asked.

"Yes, the boy returned it on his own."

"Was there anything missing?"

"No, nothing is missing. All my money is still there, credit cards too. It all happened so fast, I don't think there was time to go through it."

"Okay," he said. He opened up a little pad of paper and took down their names, addresses, and phone numbers.

The tall man wouldn't be ignored any longer. "I saw the whole thing too, you know. Maybe he didn't take the wallet, but he accepted it and isn't receiving stolen property illegal?"

The other cop asked him. "But you agree the young man we have in custody did not steal the wallet, correct?"

"His friend did, but he took it and ran away. I caught that scumbag. I watched him. I knew they were up to no good. I know a rat when I see one! He's an accomplice! You should be happy I caught one of those…those…hoods!"

"Sir, please lower your voice," the cop said blandly, as if he was used to dealing with such arrogant tools all the time. Danny would have looked for a reason to put him in one of those Hannibal Lecter muzzles from that movie—just to get the guy to clam up. Instead, the cop asked him, "I'll take the descriptions on the others you saw with him, but I can't promise we'll find them."

This seemed to give the miffed man something to do that he enjoyed—playing narc on homeless teens.

"What's going to happen?" Danny asked his father.

"I don't know."

The officers spoke quietly together while the boy stared forlornly from the back of the patrol car. The crowd started to dissipate, more interested in finding a good deal than watching them now that the show was over. Danny shifted from one foot to another, ready to walk away with a story to tell, but not wanting to see an obvious innocent person arrested for something someone else did.

The heavier officer waved Marvin over and said, "Your story matches what the kid's saying. If you press charges, we'll process him and try to get in touch with his folks. He came back clean, no wants or warrants. It's up to you. What do you want to do?"

"Don't let him get away with it!" The tall man snarled a curse. "Evil happens when good men do nothing. You gonna let him go and rob other people now? That'll be on your head!"

"Hey, cool down," the smaller officer said, stepping close to the man. "We got your witness statement. There's nothing more for you to do here."

"What do you want to do?" The other officer asked again, obviously eager to get back to more important things.

They stared at the kid with the dark brown hair and despairing eyes. That kid's been through a lot, Danny thought, knowing his father would think the same but wanted to hear him say it. "You're not pressing charges, are you, Dad?"

"No," he said with a sigh. "I guess not."

"Okay, then. We're all done here." The officer opened the back door to the police car and let the kid out.

The tall man waved at us in disgust and walked away mumbling angrily to himself. Few sandwiches short of a picnic, Danny thought, glad to see the guy go. The remaining onlookers seemed to feel the same because a collective sigh of relief passed amongst them as they turned back to hunting up that perfect treasure or great deal.

As they headed back to the Porsche, the bigger officer caught up to them. "Here," he said, offering a small card. "If you change your mind or run across the kid who did take your wallet, you can get me at these numbers. I put the boy's info on the back in case he turns up again, but I don't think you'll have any more problems with him."

Marvin took the card and Danny read over his shoulder; *Andy Riley. 256 Colonial Avenue, Newport News.* His father tucked it into his wallet as he said, "Thanks officer, for your time."

"Have a good day," he said and returned to his partner.

"Newport News is close by us. You think he came all this way by himself?" Danny asked.

"I don't' know, but let's just hope he doesn't get into anymore trouble."

They walked in silence for a few minutes then Marvin

asked, "Did he remind you of Ryan at all?"

Danny shook his head as they reached the Porsche. "No. They don't look anything alike."

"You probably don't remember," his father said as the top lowered and they got in. "You were so young. Well, you both were. When Ryan first came to live with us, he had that same sort of look in his eyes. Like he'd been hurt so bad that he would never be the same again."

Danny didn't want to talk about how bad Ryan had it before coming to live with them. He felt for his friend, they were practically brothers after all. Dwelling on Ryan's past though, made him uncomfortable and angry. Some people just shouldn't have kids.

CHAPTER 12

The Lost Boy

Caught in traffic, the Porsche inched back toward the interstate. With Ryan on his way out to go bowling in a few hours, Danny hoped the traffic would let up soon so they'd have time to grab a bite to eat before heading out.

"This is crazy."

Danny yawned, more hungry than tired, but the back seat called to him. More than once he'd lain in the back, staring at the sky as they rode along—well, until he fell asleep with the sun shining on his face. "I'm gonna go in the back, Dad."

"Okay." His father turned his blinker on and headed toward an alley. "I know a short cut through here."

Danny settled against the seat and closed his eyes, unsure if shortcut really meant shortcut or if he'd wake up that night well-rested, but starving at the bowling alley without ever having made it home.

The sound of the Porsche's fine-tuned engine changed as they passed into the shadowy corridor between the tall buildings. He sensed them crossing a street and then heading into another alley. When he peeked, the broad expanse of steel and concrete rising up into a blue sky with billowy white clouds proved him right.

"Oh no," his father said, his voice dropping an octave.

"What's up?" Danny asked sitting up as the car came to a halt.

"Those are the same kids, aren't they?"

Ahead, in the alley, number twenty-four, the Andy kid from the flea market, was on the ground, the kid in the leather coat kicking him while the one with the skateboard watched the street at the other end of the alley. Before Danny could agree they were the same kids, his father revved the engine, then squealed tires, shooting forward like an action movie come to life.

Holy crap!

Danny grabbed the back of his father's seat. Grimy-haired leather-boy looked up, the surprise on his face almost comical. He spun on his cowboy heel and ran toward the guy with the skateboard. For a heart stopping moment, Danny freaked that they might not stop in time and run over Andy.

The car halted so fast, Danny was thrown into the back of his father's seat. By the time he straightened, his dad was out of the car and kneeling on the ground by Andy. The kid's nose was bleeding and a bruise was already forming on his cheekbone. He looked rough.

"Are you okay?" Marvin asked.

He wiped his bloody nose with the back of his hand. "I'm okay. Are you gonna call the police?"

"Only if you want me to." He stood and held a hand out.

Andy took the hand and let Marvin help to his feet, rubbing at the blood on his nose. "You're not gonna report me? Like that other guy wanted you to?"

"That guy's probably out there yelling about something else by now. To me it was over when I got my wallet back. I didn't call the police in the first place. You said you didn't know what they were up to and I was okay with that," Marvin called back to the car, "Danny, grab those tissues from the glove box. He's bleeding pretty good over here."

Danny grabbed the little travel package of tissues, got out of the car and handed them to Andy. "Here you go."

"Thanks," he said, leaving blood smears on the package as he coaxed a few tissues out. Up close, he seemed thinner and younger under the oversized jersey.

"What were you doing with those kids anyway?" Marvin asked.

Andy shrugged. "Don't know. They were just...there, sort of."

Danny raised his eyebrows at his father. Weird answer. He must be some kind of a runaway or something, which meant his home life probably sucked.

"Some friends you got there, you really need to be more careful about who you hang out with."

He held the tissue to his nose, speaking through the wad. "I don' wanna see dem eva again."

"Well good," Marvin said. He smiled and offered with a chuckle, "Guess that's the second time I saved you today. That's once more than I normally offer for free. Next time I'll have to bill you."

His tissue came away with less blood than before and he offered a shy smile in return. "I'm sorry I caused you guys all that trouble earlier."

"Hey, you didn't cause me any trouble." Danny didn't know exactly why, but he wanted to cheer the guy up. No one deserved to get beaten up like that.

140

"And you helped me when you gave my wallet back. If one of them had it, I'd be canceling my credit cards right now."

"I didn't know they were gonna rob people. I ran away because I didn't know what else to do." More tissues came out, though the blood slowed to a mere trickle.

Marvin asked, "Your name's Andy right?"

"Yeah, how'd you know?"

"The cops gave me your information in case I changed my mind."

"I'm glad you didn't," Andy said. He glanced at Danny, then back at Marvin. "I don't want to cause more trouble, but you think I could get a ride somewhere, like a gas station or something so I can get cleaned up?"

Danny cast a quick glance at his father, a man well known for helping people with problems. His dad just couldn't walk away from a situation he knew he could make better. Admirable, but a real pain too. They were supposed to be heading home, not playing chauffer for some homeless kid. He grimaced, feeling like a jerk for having not so nice thoughts.

For once though, Marvin seemed to notice that even though this one looked harmless enough, he could be hiding a gun, maybe want to carjack the Porsche. "I'm sorry. We're running really late. Is there someone you can call? You can use my cell phone if you like."

Andy looked at them with humongous hazel blue eyes like some ad for Save the Seals or something. "Those guys might come back for me. I swear I'm not a bad kid. I never got in trouble before. Please don't leave me here, sir?"

Marvin took the phone out of his pocket. "How about if I call someone for you?"

Andy lowered his head. "Never mind, you're no different than everybody else."

"Sorry, I really don't feel right giving a ride to a stranger. Please understand, I have my son with me. You should get going in case they do come back."

Danny didn't object to the suggestion he needed to be protected from the kid because he didn't really want to give Andy a ride and if using the excuse of having him along worked, he didn't mind.

Andy leaned against the wall and shoved his hands in his pockets. Drying blood smeared across his cheek like war paint. "I don't care. Whatever. I'll probably end up in a hospital or dead when they get done with me, but at least people get paid to care then."

Danny held his breath, watching his father turn green with guilt. To his surprise though, Marvin slumped and headed back to the car.

"Get in," he said softly to Danny.

Now he felt like a real loser. They were gonna leave a poor bloody kid alone in an alley when all he wanted was to find a place to clean up. As he climbed into the backseat, Danny's stomach growled again and he wondered when the last time that scrawny kid had eaten a decent meal. Jeez, he thought, I'm getting as bad as my dad.

Marvin started the car and eased down the length of the alley. Danny watched Andy grow smaller and smaller as they reached the opposite end. When they turned right instead of left, he had the sinking feeling he knew what his father was doing.

"I just want to drive around the block, make sure he's not still just sitting there," Marvin muttered barely loud enough for Danny to know he was talking to him.

Stopped at a light, he felt an urgency he didn't like. They couldn't save all the kids in the world. Yeah, he thought, but we shouldn't just walk away when we can offer a little help. "You're going to give him a ride, aren't you Dad?"

He didn't answer as the light turned green and traffic moved forward, allowing him to make another right turn. Danny sat up, intent on moving to the front seat because by now, he was ready to bank on his father giving Andy a lift, but he stopped as the Porsche slowed almost imperceptibly as Marvin saw the same thing he did.

Skater boy and Cowboy boots kid, who carried a big stick, turned back into the alley. They must have been waiting for them to drive away, watching for their moment to return. The sheer malice of that intention made Danny angry. Screw them.

Engine howling, his dad raced forward and yanked the wheel hard. He stomped on the gas again. Tires squealed as the rear broke out slightly. They came to a stop at the mouth of the alley. This time, the boys didn't look ready to run. They looked ready for a fight. Andy stood in front of them, sweaty and pale.

Marvin pushed the passenger door open. "Get in!"

"Hurry," Danny shouted.

Andy moved quickly to avoid the swinging stick and more fell into the seat then sat down. He yanked the door closed as a rock whizzed by over their heads.

Danny glanced back. Skater boy had dropped his board and was hefting another rock the size of a tomato. "Dad, go!"

He floored it, throwing Danny back against the seat and Andy off balance as the kid struggled to grab his seatbelt.

Something hit the back of the car, but it wasn't loud or hard enough to have been the rock the skater had. In the street behind them, lay the stick Boots had swung at Andy. The two boys stood in the middle of the street shouting something Danny couldn't hear and throwing more rocks and road debris that couldn't reach them. He twisted back in his seat. "Holy cow, that was intense!"

"Put your seatbelts on," Marvin ordered.

Danny did so without pointing out that it might have been more prudent to ask them to do that before he slowed down. Now wasn't the time to bust his chops though.

Andy put his seatbelt on and said, "They were crazy. They could have seriously messed up your car."

His father drove for a moment, thinking. "Maybe you have something they want?"

He shook his head.

"Yeah," Danny said, warming to the theory. "Maybe they think you got some cash from my Dad's wallet?"

Andy actually blushed. "They didn't believe me when I said I gave it all back. Thought I ratted them out to the cops and that's why I didn't get arrested."

"Well," Marvin said, turning to smile at the kid as they stopped in the traffic getting onto the interstate. "Looks like I've got a third rescue in me after all. No charge, considering I got my wallet and everything in it back safe and sound thanks to you."

The whole situation was crazy. As the large buildings turned into hotels and fast-food chains, his father's shortcut making little difference in their speed, Danny thought the kid had a black cloud hanging over his head. Framed for a theft he didn't commit, manhandled by a wacko, stuffed in the back of a cruiser then just when it seemed nothing else bad would happen, he got beaten up by a bunch of street thugs. Definitely a bad day.

Instead of getting on the interstate, Marvin drove through the green light and onto the boulevard, heading toward a chain of restaurants lighting up the street like Vegas in the darkening afternoon. The storm they'd left back home headed their way, thick roiling clouds off in the distance. A deep purplish black meant rain was more than just a probability. The golden glow of twin arches against that backdrop made his stomach gurgle again. "Hey, can we stop for a burger? I'm starving."

Andy jerked in his seat and glanced at him with horror-stricken eyes, then just as quickly, turned to face forward again.

"Yeah, I'm hungry too," Marvin said. "How about it? You got time for a burger?"

Andy didn't answer and Danny feared they'd ride past all the restaurants before he did. Finally, he said, "I don't have any money."

"My treat," Marvin said. "In fact, I know of this great place up the road I used to go to all the time when I lived here."

Once they parked, Danny waited for Andy to get out.

The kid went to the back of the car and inspected the paint.

"Aww, man, they chipped the paint. I can't believe they threw stuff at us. This is so bad." Totally beside himself, he stumbled away, hands on his head. "So bad."

Marvin said, "Don't worry, that was there before."

"Yeah," Danny said. "Only a stick hit the back bumper, and not hard enough to do any damage."

"Really?" Relief flooded his face.

"Yep. So let's get something to eat, okay?" Marvin bent inside and pushed the button to raise the top again. "I can smell the rain coming."

Danny inhaled the fresh taste of clean rain coming on the currents generated by the far off storm. The breeze gusted a bit harder, cooler. It felt good.

Andy watched the top rise, eyes wide. "Wow. It's electric?"

Marvin smiled across to Danny, then said to Andy, "Yes. You hungry?"

"Starving," Andy said, grinning ear to ear.

Danny stood beside him as his father led the way to the door and held it open. The foul stench coming off Andy was so intense he could almost touch it with his bare hands. With the hood up on the Porsche, riding home was going to be harsh.

CHAPTER 13

Burgers and Bad Boys

One geezer sat in the corner eating a burger and drinking coffee. The combo seemed gross to Danny, but not nearly as bad as Andy's *Eu de Stink-o.*

"I'm so glad this place is still here. Used to come in all the time when I lived down here." His father grinned one of those infectious kinds and even Andy smiled in return. "What would you like?"

"Whatever you think is good." His solemn gaze traveled hungrily over the menu.

"Go ahead, pick something," Marvin said, reaching for his wallet.

Maybe they did owe Andy a little bit of a reward after all. Heck, if the kid hadn't returned the wallet, they'd be waiting until they got home to eat. Danny's empty stomach thanked him with a grumble of appreciation.

When Andy didn't respond, he tried not to inhale too much of his stench as he placed his order. His father ordered, the kid beside him almost green around the gills, his hunger so obvious.

"Don't worry about the price," Marvin said. "Whatever you want. Get what looks good."

With one wary eyebrow raised, Andy asked, "Are you sure?"

"Yeah, don't worry, get anything you want."

The skinny blonde cashier with big metal braces hid her boredom with a lukewarm smile. "Are you ready to order now?"

"Two double cheeseburgers no pickles, one large bacon burger no lettuce, a large Pepsi and medium fries."

"Is this for here, or to go?"

"For here," Marvin answered.

Danny headed to the condiment station and gathered napkins, needing a reason to be as far away as politely possible from Andy. The kid had himself a massive dose of bad B.O., he thought, thankful he didn't have to live with him.

At the counter, where they waited for the food, Marvin asked, "Everything okay, Andy?"

Danny listened, filling up the little paper tubs with ketchup. The pump nearly empty, it sputtered as he slapped it. The smell of French fries made his stomach gurgle again, singing chorus with the ketchup pump.

His dad asked, "What are you doing in Virginia Beach? Family?"

"I don't have any family here."

Jeez, could he be any more pitiful? That would play on his dad's heartstrings for sure.

"I'm sorry I didn't offer you a ride at first," his dad said. "If I'd a known they were hanging around, waiting for you, I would have given you a lift right away."

"That's all right." He made no hail out of it and the food came, postponing anymore chatter until they were all seated.

He must have been starving because he finished the first

cheeseburger with only four bites. "Sorry," he said around his bulging cheek. "These are *so* good!"

While Danny dipped a fry in ketchup, Andy bit into the next burger like one of those starving dogs on an animal rescue show. When was the last time he ate?

His dad remained uncharacteristically quiet. Danny didn't care much for the awkward silence and said, "Dude, where do you go to school?"

"Not sure," he mumbled around a cheek full of food. "We're moving."

"I'd hate that. I'm gonna be a senior this year and it would bite big dog turds if we had to move."

"Danny," his father scolded, though his eyes twinkled. "Not so gross while I'm eating, hey?"

"Sorry." Danny grinned and bit into his burger. "But it would."

Andy asked, "Where do you guys live?"

"In Hampton. I haven't been down here in a while. I used to live here, but that was years ago."

"You're from Hampton, for real? Newport News is right by you."

"We're practically neighbors, hey?" Marvin wiped his hands on a napkin, balled up the wrapper from his burger, and asked, "So what do your folks doing for a living?"

Andy sucked on his soda, swallowed hard, and said, "Well, my dad's a truck driver. He drives huge semi trucks, all up and down the east coast and my mom works for the newspaper. My parents make good money. My dad is like one of the best drivers they have and my mom has fifteen people working under her. She's really good at what she does."

"Ever go on the road with your dad? See some cool places?" Danny asked. How cool would it be if his father was a trucker? They could go all over the U.S., maybe even into Canada or Mexico.

Andy wiped one hand on the side of his jeans, pulled a picture out of his back pocket, and showed it to them. He and his father stood next to a bright red semi. "I wanted to go with my dad, but then…well…I went to Syracuse with my friend Jason and his parents. I just got back a few days ago. Syracuse was awesome. I went fishing like every day with my friend Jason. Do you ever go fishing? I love it, I could go every day."

"Danny and I used to go every weekend, but we haven't been in a while. He has a job now so it's tough to get away. That's a good idea though. We should go soon. Maybe you can take a day off or swap shifts with someone."

Fishing could either be tons of fun, or the most boring day of his life, all depended on if the fish were biting. The guy who wrote up the schedules at the Food Lion could be a real jerk though. "I'll check."

"I'll turn eighteen in November and I can go where I want then. I'll go fishing with you, if you take me?"

His dad gave Danny an odd look, like he wanted help, but he gave him a little shrug. What was he supposed to do, make up an excuse why his father couldn't take him along?

"Sure, if we go," Marvin said. "I don't see why you couldn't come along."

"But you'd have to pick me up, because you know I don't have a car," he asked Danny. "Do you drive?"

150

"Yeah." Danny drank from his straw. "I'm hoping Dad's gonna help me get a better car soon though. Hint, hint."

Marvin smiled and started piling up their garbage. "We'll see, we'll see."

"That's cool. I don't have my license yet, but I'll get it soon, and a guy who works with my mom is going to sell me his 2002 RSX for like two-thousand dollars. I'm going to get me a custom paint job."

"Dude, that's cheap. Is it a stick?"

"No, it's an Acura," Andy said, and laughed. "What's a stick?"

Danny chuffed. "A *manual* transmission, dude. Y'know, with a clutch where you have to shift the gears manually?"

Andy's eyebrows rose to the sky.

"All right, let me put it this way. Does it have a five speed manual transmission or does the car have an automatic transmission?"

"It's a stick shift." Andy smiled like he had known all along. He shoved the last bite of burger in his cheek and asked Marvin, "I like your Porsche, if you ever sell that, I want it. That's my dream car."

Get in line, buddy, Danny thought, but didn't say anything. The chances Andy would get the car before him were slim to no way.

As they finished with sighs of satisfaction, Marvin stared, as if unsure what to do next. Danny didn't understand his hesitation at first, but then his dad said, "Well, Andy, I hope you have a better day."

Oh yeah, even more awkward now. Danny stood with his father, grabbing the tray of trash.

"So you gotta go now?" Andy rose and put his hand out. As Marvin shook it, he said, "Thanks for the food. I hadn't eaten in like forever."

Marvin's face clouded. "Are you sure you're gonna be alright?"

He nodded. "I'll have somebody pick me up. Thanks again it was nice meeting you."

Danny gave him a wave as he shoved the trash through the swinging door on the bin. Two police officers, their radios squawking came in and walked straight to the counter. Not the same two from earlier, but one threw a quick glance at Andy as if he could smell the stench of runaway on him.

"There've been some complaints up the road about a bunch kids causing trouble. You have any trouble?" A tall redheaded cop asked the girl behind the counter.

Danny got nervous, feeling stupid for the mini-freak. Couldn't be the same kids from the flea market, right? But what if Andy was in some sort of gang and this was all a set up to get free food and maybe carjack the Porsche? Danny glanced out the window. The Porsche waited for them, untouched, the blue deepening as the coming storm darkened the reflection.

Andy broke out in a sweat and slid a sidelong glance at the police. The three of them stood there, like jewelry thieves wearing ski masks and holding black velvet bags.

Brace-face said, "Nope, just the two kids over there, but they aren't bothering anyone."

The police officer turned to look at them then eyed the old guy in the corner still sipping his coffee as he read a newspaper. The officer's started for them, his hand on his

152

belt, resting, but ready. "That your Porsche out there?"

"Yes," Marvin croaked, then cleared his throat. "That's mine, I mean."

"That's a really nice car."

"Thanks," he said, his smile nervous as he held out his arms to usher them both toward the car. "Well, boys, you ready to go?"

Andy didn't catch what Marvin was up to and stopped on the spot and stared at him as if he had gone crazy.

He put his arm out to push the door open when the officer stopped them in their tracks "Sir, just a second!"

They turned together. It would have been comical if the situation hadn't been so intense. Danny, slightly behind Andy, breathed through his mouth.

The cop asked, "You seen any kids running the streets around here?"

Andy turned tomato red and he shook his head.

Danny just swallowed, trying to think what might happen if his dad got arrested for picking up a minor. Once they learned he did foster care and worked trouble kids before, they probably would be all right about it, but still, bailing his father out of jail wasn't high on his list of things to do before he died.

"No officer." Marvin smiled, to Danny's disbelief. "But I'll keep an eye out and report anything."

"What happened to his face?" The cop asked, jerking his chin toward Andy.

"He had hockey practice," Danny blurted, hoping the word liar wasn't flashing in neon over his head.

The police officer studied them for a moment. "Just be

careful out there."

"We will." Marvin opened the door.

They rushed outside and got in the car. Since Andy couldn't figure out how to pop the seat forward and climb in the back, Danny hurried into the back, grimacing as he passed near Andy's armpit. Ugh!

"Buckle up." Marvin nodded to the watching cop.

Danny made a big show of putting on his seatbelt. His dad waved goodbye to the officer who waved back and watched until they were out of the parking lot.

His heart rate returned to normal, but he wanted to peek at the road behind them. He asked, "You think they were looking for those guys from the alley?"

"That'd be my guess," Marvin said.

Andy glanced over his shoulder, out the rear window, then back at Marvin. "For real...you think they noticed anything?"

"Hard to say, we're not being followed."

"Oh crap, now what am I gonna do?"

"I think I should take you home, before you end up in the backseat of one of those patrol cars again. You might not be so lucky next time."

Andy looked out the rear window again, his gaze meeting Danny's before quickly darting away. "All right...Yeah I better get back. But I didn't do anything!"

"Sometimes, that doesn't matter."

Danny sighed then tried to bury his nose in his t-shirt as he inhaled. How could his dad stand it, sitting up there with him?

They sped onto the I-264 onramp. The Porsche growled,

gnashing against the stranglehold of second gear. His dad pushed the rpm's to 4000, kept her there steady. How he loved that sound. If he got the Porsche, he'd drive her on the interstate just to hear it again.

They buzzed by slower drivers and entered the acceleration lane. Slowing down behind those cars would be a sin in a Porsche. He pushed the pedal all the way, and Danny loved the thrill. The rpm needle raced to 7000, pulling them with an evil roar in front of all the traffic.

Andy laughed. "Holy crap, this car is fast! They couldn't catch us in this car, could they?"

Danny chuckled. "Dad won't run from the cops. He'll just psych them out and wave goodbye."

"I know, right?" Andy asked, turning so he could talk to Danny. "It was so cool when he acted like I was his kid and you said that thing about hockey. I didn't get it at first, I thought I was losing it, but it was awesome!"

"I feel kind of guilty, though. I wish I would have thought to have you tell him what you knew, you know, help them out with their investigation and everything?" Marvin asked, "So, do you know those other guys by name?"

"One was Rick, the other I forgot, John or Johnny I think."

They wove in and out of traffic, the engine running mean and deep.

"I've never gone this fast in my life," Andy said. "How fast does it go?"

"I don't know I never got over one-twenty with her."

Andy fell quiet after that and Danny lay back as the first drops of rain splattered across the windshield. His dad cracked the window, offering the excuse that he loved the smell of rain, which was true. But, if you asked Danny, he did it to vent Andy's odor, and he totally appreciated that. As he had the thought, a bucketful of guilt landed on him. This kid, for whatever reason, had experienced the worst day he had ever witnessed and here he was, griping about a bad smell in the air. He hadn't been beaten up. He hadn't been almost arrested and shaken by a strange man. Without thinking it through, Danny asked, "Ever been bowling?"

Andy yawned. "Just once."

"We're going tonight," Danny said, catching a sharp look from his dad in the mirror. "Maybe if your folks say it's okay, you could come with us. I don't have to work tomorrow, I could run you back."

He didn't answer, his profile serene, eyes closed and Danny wondered if the kid could have fallen asleep while he was asking. He yawned again and answered, "Don't got anyone to ask," he paused and added, "There's nobody waiting for me anyway. My parents are dead. No one will miss me."

CHAPTER 14

Confessions of a Teenage Orphan

Danny sat up and leaned between the seats, ignoring the sweat and funk smell coming off him. "Huh? Your parents are dead? Like in buried or just like dead to you 'cause you're mad at them?"

Marvin turned, his eyebrows creased with true concern, eyes full of empathy. "Are you alone?"

If he had been sleepy, he wasn't anymore. Caught in their attention he shifted nervously, rolling a cuff between two fingers. "Yeah. I don't have a home anymore. I'm sorry I wasn't completely honest with you. Mom and Dad are dead and nobody's at my house. Only our stuff is in there."

"How did they die?" Marvin asked, slowing and moving toward the right lane.

Danny sat back, stunned. He didn't think he'd ever met an orphan before. Oh jeez, he was really gonna burn now after all those mean thoughts he had.

"Dad died five years ago. Dropped dead on the spot from a heart attack. No warning, nothing." Andy shuddered a little bit and when he spoke again, his voice cracked. "Mom, she was on a trip with this guy and I guess they crashed bad. That was last week and now I have nobody and I don't know where home is anymore. Maybe if I hadn't left, maybe my mom wouldn't have gone on the trip. I didn't want her to, but I let her go anyway. She would still be alive if it weren't for me. It's all my fault that she's dead now."

"Your mom just died a week ago? Oh man, I'm sorry." Danny's own mom was out in California with her new husband and three little half-sisters he'd never met. She left when he was a kid and he saw her maybe once every five years. He didn't know what it would be like to lose her because he didn't feel like he ever really had her anyway. He would be upset, right? Wouldn't he?

If he lost his dad though, that would blow him away. It was just the two of them against the world and it had been since his mom left. He couldn't imagine life without him.

Marvin asked, "Are you staying with someone?"

"Nobody. I don't know if there's anyone at my house. My aunt maybe...I don't know, I haven't been there since the day I found out she died. I went a little crazy, knocked some stuff around. I took the picture of me and my dad and left." He could barely get out the words.

Marvin turned the blinker on to take the next exit and said, "It's not your fault Andy. Don't blame yourself."

"Yes, it is. See I was in Syracuse with my friend Jason. I had to fly home. I didn't believe she died. I searched through the whole house. She wasn't there. I tried her cell phone, but the voicemail came on, that's when I freaked out. I haven't been back since. I don't even know if my mom was buried." He sobbed.

Marvin pulled to the shoulder and stopped. He patted Andy's back awkwardly and gave Danny a sympathetic look.

Danny didn't know what to do. Tears always made him uncomfortable. Like he was looking at something he wasn't supposed to see, like it was private. He wanted to tell the kid it would be okay, but jeez, it wouldn't be okay for him, would it?

When Andy could speak again, he said, "See I went to Syracuse 'cause my mom and I had an argument about this guy Gary who was probably driving. I only said I'd go with Jason 'cause I was mad at my mom. So you see it was my fault."

Danny didn't know what to say, but felt obligated to say something. How could he show him how bad he felt for him? He wanted to cheer him up or something, but could only remotely imagine what it must be like losing both his mom and dad.

Marvin handed Andy what was left of the tissues. They came away smeared a little brown, a left over from getting beat up, Danny guessed.

"I lost both my parents too. They passed recently, pretty much of old age. But I can't imagine how you're holding up. I don't know if I would have been strong enough to cope at your age," Marvin said as Andy finished cleaning his face. "Where have you been this whole time?"

"I don't know, running around I guess, I don't remember what all I did, I don't even remember how I got to Virginia Beach. I don't care either. Isn't it silly how I forgot?"

"Naw," Danny said. "I saw a thing on detectives trying to figure out why a whole bunch of people can remember the same thing a hundred different ways. They said it happens when we get really upset. Our brain can like erase your memories or something, to protect us from whatever freaked us out to begin with."

"I remember when my dad died," Andy said. "Never sick in his life. Didn't smoke or drink and he wasn't that old. I was 'sposed to go with him that summer. On my first trip ever. You know what my mom said when she told me? *You have to be strong now.* That's what she said. That I had to be strong.

"I stopped talking for a while. My mom said it broke her heart. She was all I had and now she's dead too. I don't know what to do anymore. I'm too scared to go home. What's gonna happen to me now? I don't want to go to some orphanage, but I'm not old enough to stay by myself."

The rain cocooned them inside the Porsche, creating their own private world hidden away from everyone. Danny wondered if he could ever talk so openly with strangers. Heck, he had a tough time with his best friends and family.

Marvin put a hand on the boy's shoulder. "They don't put kids your age in homes anymore. Worst case scenario they place you with foster parents, but only if there is absolutely no family fit or willing to take you in."

"Nobody wants me. Maybe my aunt in Baltimore, but I don't want to move to Baltimore. There's nobody else."

"Let's talk more at my house." Marvin put the Porsche in first. "Give me a chance to think."

"Dad's great at finding stuff out. He's been a foster parent before, so he knows what he's doing." That was the best Danny could offer in the way of comfort. He hoped it helped him feel more at ease. Seriously. They could have been serial killers for all Andy knew and here he was, on the way to their house. Somebody had to look out for the guy. He obviously couldn't do that on his own.

The grief seeping from the passenger seat made the air feel heavy and oppressive. He watched the side of the road, trying not to breathe in the human fumes and waiting impatiently for every landmark on the way home. The Food Lion where he worked, the gas station where his neighborhood started. The dead tree in someone's yard he always expected to be lying across the road one day. Then they were parking in the garage and he could hardly wait for Andy to get out so he could follow.

The rain was a mere drizzle and warm, sliding through his hair and cooling his scalp as he waited for his dad to unlock the door. Andy hung back a little, staring at the driveway and the street beyond, as if contemplating how quickly he could run away. He stepped in after them though and when Marvin gestured to a chair at the kitchen table, asking him to sit, he did.

Danny kicked off his sneakers and headed for the sofa. In the kitchen, he heard his dad filling the coffee maker and guessed this would be one of the kitchen-table-talks they had every now and then when things got seriously important.

He flipped the television on, keeping the volume low so he could hear but not appear like he was eavesdropping. If his dad wanted him at the table, he'd call him in, but for the most part, Marvin preferred those talks to be one-on-one.

Andy stood and came to stare at an international eating competition in Japanese. "Look at that guy. What a complete dork. I like cheese, but even I couldn't eat that much at once."

"Yeah," Danny said. "Once saw a guy eat like twenty cheeseburgers at Burger King. Big fat guy. Drove a Moped."

He snorted. "Bet he had to super-charge that thing."

"Yeah," he said and switched the channel. A rerun of a cop show came on, the police running after some kid in a white t-shirt at night in a trashy neighborhood. "Think they'll catch him?"

"Probably," Andy said. "Y'know, I can't believe those guys threw rocks at your dad's car. I wish the cops would have caught them."

Danny grunted. The kid on television tried to hop a fence, but the middle-aged dude, breathing so hard you could hardly hear anything else, snatched the back of the kid's shirt and flung him back into a bunch of bushes. They all disappeared from the light of the camera.

"Your dad was so cool. He came tearing up the road, squealing tires and everything, just like in the movies."

Danny smiled. "He's that sort of guy."

"Wish…well, never mind." He stretched, releasing the full glory of his pit smell. "He could probably be a stunt man. Maybe work in Hollywood. Maybe I could do that, if I had a car like his. Make a million dollars. You know, work with all the big action actors like that guy the Rock or whatever. Could you see it? That blue Porsche flying up and down those hills like in the movies. Maybe a ton of cops chasing and no one can catch us.

"Or yeah, maybe a bunch of guys with like machine guns trying to shoot out my tires and I could really hammer it like your dad did on the way home. That's a really sweet car. You think he'll ever sell it?"

He said it with such excitement and hope that Danny didn't want to tell him he had dibs on the wheels and said instead, "Never know what he'll do."

"I know! I'd be sitting in jail if it weren't for him. The way your dad played it off, like I was his kid in front of those other cops was way cool. So smooth. I can't ever be that smooth. I get all nervous and stuff. Pretty much suck at it. I don't think I've sweated so much in my whole life."

Oh Danny wasn't so sure about that. The kid smelled like he had sweated a few too many times in those clothes.

"Hey guys," Marvin said from the kitchen. "We should probably figure out what our plan is before it gets too late. Ryan's expecting us at the alley."

Andy shrank, maybe two years and two sizes. The kid had real issues, Danny thought. "You're still going with us, right?"

"I think he needs to at least call someone and let them know where he's at," Marvin said, sipping from a steaming mug of coffee. "Can you think of anyone you could let know where you are? A neighbor or something?"

Andy shook his head.

If there was one thing Danny had learned all these years with one foster brother after another, it was that sudden guilt gave everyone the same expression—those who weren't good liars anyway. Andy did have someone to call, but not someone he would call.

"Well," Marvin said, moving toward the stairs to the second floor. "If you want to get washed up, you can use the bathroom downstairs. Danny, loan him a shirt if he wants, okay?"

"No problem." He flipped the station as one of those birth control pill commercials came on and while an announcer went on about how the stuff could kill you the actresses all smiled and smelled flowers.

His dad headed up the stairs, probably to make some phone calls of his own and check email. Just because he didn't go after Andy to spill the beans about who to call right then and there, didn't mean he had given up. Heck, if Danny tried, he could probably get Andy to tell him everything. "So what do you like to watch at home?"

He shrugged. "Nothing much."

"Yeah, a zillion channels and nothing on, right?"

"Yeah," Andy said. "Think I'll wash up now."

"'Kay," Danny said and stood. "My room's upstairs. I'll get you a shirt."

"Thanks."

Danny hopped up the stairs and hurried into his room. If they were gonna go bowling together, he didn't want Ryan to die from inhaling that toxic odor. He rummaged through his drawer for the green t-shirt that had started getting too small on him, now that he'd grown like half a foot. Shirt in hand, he went back into the hall, listening for the sound of running water in the walls when someone turned on the faucet in the bathroom downstairs.

Instead, he heard voices coming from his dad's office.

Marvin said, "She's gonna worry about you."

"I know," he said low, almost too quiet to hear. "But she's not really gonna care, not really. I barely even know her."

"Still, I'd feel better knowing she wasn't worrying about you."

He said something Danny couldn't hear then said, "Just

one. Please. I'll call in the morning."

Silence.

He couldn't predict what his dad would do. Sometimes he could be a stickler for court and legal type stuff, other times he bent rules practically in two.

Marvin said, "All right. Just one night, but we'll have to get you home tomorrow.

"Cool," he said, "Thanks. Really thanks a lot."

Andy was like an emotional Transformer, one minute all guilty and down and the next, grinning like a rich guy in a videogame store. Yet even as he smiled, underneath that cheery façade lurked a butt load of troubles. Even Darth Vader would have felt for the kid.

CHAPTER 15

The Haunted House

"That kid is totally messed up," Danny said once Andy was locked in the downstairs bathroom and the water started running. He'd given him a full set of clothes, adding jogging pants to the shirt. "You think he'll leave sludge in the shower? Man, did he stink."

"He's probably been living on the street for a while." His dad sat across from him at the kitchen table. The rain had stopped, but the world glistened wetly beyond the window. "He seems to feel comfortable around you though. That's good."

"What did you guys talk about when I was digging out more clothes for him?"

Marvin shrugged. "It's weird. He's obviously crazy with grief about his mom but it's hard to believe he doesn't know if she's been buried."

"He sure wasn't in a hurry to call and find out."

"Sometimes, knowing can be harder than not knowing. Maybe he's just not ready to face that."

They sat quietly for a moment. "Yeah, if he lost his dad, like he says, and now his mom, that's gotta be super tough."

Marvin nodded. "Explains too, why he can remember flying on the plane, and how long ago he got back. Couldn't have been more than a few days, I'm guessing. He was rank, but he didn't look like he'd gotten used to living out there by himself."

Danny had another thought. "You think he's gonna get his driving permit now, without his mom? Or that car he wanted from that guy she worked with? He seemed really stoked about that."

"Probably not until he's placed, either with a relative or in a home."

Normally, Danny got a bit of eye rolling when his dad took on another foster kid. So many had shown up with an attitude. Even if it didn't last long, it could be a total downer. Andy, on the other hand, kept reminding him of that lost puppy who'd been kicked or hit by a car and was found licking his wounds in the gutter, still trying to wag his tail. He couldn't just walk away, no one could. "Maybe you could help him out, Dad. At least help him get his permit. We could use my car and get him some driving time in."

He frowned. "We'll see. It might not be as simple as that. If he turns out to be on the run, and I'm letting him stay here tonight without gaining permission, we could be harboring a runaway and that's against the law."

"So you're going to turn him in?" Danny didn't know why, but that made him mad. After all the kids his father had helped, and after all Andy had already been through, turning him in now was like quitting the race before you even ran out of breath.

"No. But I can't let him stay indefinitely without permission. We're going to have to get him to see how important it is to do this the right way."

"So you are gonna take him in?"

167

"I didn't say that either." He smiled, crossed his arms, and leaned back. "What is it with you and this boy? It normally takes you at least a week to warm up to a new kid in the house and you're already playing advocate here."

Danny felt his face warm and leaned back too, trying to figure out how he could tell his dad about the puppy thing. In a way, though, it was more than that. About the time he started high school, Marvin had stopped taking kids in. He never said so, but Danny guessed he was afraid a kid who was mixed up in drugs or in trouble with the law might be a bad influence on his own son at that age. The insult of not being trusted, after practically working side by side with his dad to help out these kids his whole life, caused resentment that had simmered beneath the surface.

Plus, he was used to having someone to hang with and the house got really quiet when he was off of work and his dad was busy or out. He said, "Andy's different, don't you think? He gave you back your wallet, which would totally have never happened with some of the guys we've had living here. Except maybe with Ryan. I don't think he ever tried to swipe anything. But I don't know. Maybe I've grown up enough to see something we can help with, right? I mean, of all of them, he's probably the one that needs us the most. Did you try getting the number from the card the cop gave you?"

"It was a fake." Marvin frowned at the table and Danny could practically see the gears in his brain racing as he considered helping the kid. "I don't know yet, Danny. It might be totally out of our hands anyway."

"Yeah, but we could try. And I'm sure he'll smell a lot better now."

Marvin chuckled. "He's not like a stray dog you brought home, Danny. There are legal issues involved here."

"Never stopped us before."

He raised a brow and nodded, his expression conceding the point.

"I don't think he even knows how to take care of himself." Danny pushed.

"That's true," Marvin said. He sighed. "If I had to guess, his mom babied him after his father died. This means we have to be extra careful. If he thinks we'll take care of him in the same way, he could get hurt if we're not allowed to let him stay. Last thing that boy needs is to get hurt again."

The water in the shower went off, ending their conversation. Marvin stood. "You should get cleaned up some too. Wash up and put on a clean shirt, will ya?"

"Okay, Dad," Danny said. That was a lame-o excuse to get him out of the room. Of course he would go, because that would make it easier to eavesdrop. He made sure his footsteps sounded all the way into his room then paused, listening for the door to the downstairs bathroom to open. Backtracking silently, avoiding the squeakier spots beneath the carpeting, he knelt down at the top of the stairs, where he knew he couldn't be seen, and listened.

"Hey Andy?" Marvin asked, "Could I have your phone number? I just want to make sure there isn't anyone there worrying about you."

"Sure." The word sounded muffled, like he had a towel over his head.

The electronic beep of the number dialing was loud and Danny figured he must have put it on speaker so Andy could hear too. A recording of Andy's voice said, *"You have reached the Riley's, we can't come to the phone right now 'cause we're not at home please try again later."*

"Figured my aunt wouldn't be there," Andy said. "She probably won't even come down from Baltimore."

"What about your friend? The one you went on vacation with?"

"Jason?" Andy asked. "Naw, they probably didn't even come home and I forgot the number where they are. Besides, I think they were happy to get rid of me. They acted all weird and stuff after they got the…well, after."

"Someone has to be looking for you, wondering where you are. Maybe even afraid something bad happened to you?"

Danny held his breath, but no answer came and he figured the kid must have shaken his head or something because Marvin didn't let anyone off the hook until he had an answer. Didn't matter what the answer was, just that the answer came, because as he always said, it's rude to ignore someone talking to you.

"If we leave now, we could swing by your place on the way to the bowling alley. Then you could see if there's a letter or if someone is waiting for you? You could grab some clothes so you have something clean to put on in the morning."

"I don't want to keep your friend Ryan waiting," Andy said so softly, Danny almost didn't hear him. "Couldn't we go tomorrow?"

"It won't take long."

Danny held his breath, listening as hard as he could.

"Yeah, okay."

Good enough, Danny thought and turned back to clean up, like his father expected. Before he could come out of his room, Marvin called from the bottom of the stairs. "Danny, shake a leg. We've got a side trip to make."

"'Kay!" He called down as he finished tying his shoelace. He thundered down the stairs, grabbing a light jacket from the hook by the door as his father and Andy went into the garage. He halted on the passenger side and shrugged the jacket the rest of the way on, noticing Andy smelled a thousand times better.

"Don't worry," Danny whispered. "If there is anyone there, my dad will talk them into letting you go bowling with us. He's really good at that sort of thing."

"Okay." This time he sounded better, but not quite as excited about the night ahead as before.

The Porsche beeped twice as the alarm was disarmed and the doors unlocked. Danny leaned inside and pulled the front seat forward, grinning in his best effort to cheer him up. "C'mon, dude, hop in, and let's go."

Andy smiled, some of his spark back and leaned down to get in as Marvin slid behind the wheel.

"Hurry, I can smell the sweaty shoe rentals already." Danny gave him a friendly little shove.

"Hey," Andy said, laughing as he twisted and landed on the seat. "I'm in, I'm in. What's taking *you* so long?"

Danny laughed and snapped the seat back so he could sit down. "All right, all ready, I'm in."

"Okay boys, chill out and put your seatbelts on," Marvin said as they closed doors and did as he asked. He started the car and turned toward Newport News.

The fresh scent of shampoo was a far cry from the salty sewage odor. As it always did, when night fell, Danny experienced a surge of energy. The cooler air and bright lights, sparkling from the dampness left behind by the rain, brought life to the view. He was pumped for the night ahead and couldn't wait to tell Ryan all about their day and introduce him to Andy. If anyone could just relax the whole vibe of a room, Ryan could. Laid back, but always doing something fun, Ryan remained one of the few foster kids that really made an effort to keep in touch.

The techno thump turned up loud thrummed through him and killed any chance for a conversation. His dad most likely planned it that way so the kid couldn't try to talk him out of going to his house. He only turned the volume down when they reached Newport News and he had to rely on Andy for directions.

The neighborhood was very different than Danny expected. For some reason, he had imagined run down houses, litter everywhere, clogged gutters, and rusty junkers parked beside crumbing curbs. Instead, he found a neighborhood almost like his own. Neatly trimmed yards, empty driveways in front of closed garage doors. Porch lights shone above the front doors and big shade trees grew in every yard.

"That's it, the house with all the lights off," he said. Andy put his hands on the back of Marvin and Danny's headrests and leaned forward between them. "See? I told you there was nobody here. Can we go now please?"

Marvin pulled up to the curb. "Let's just make sure."

Andy tugged on Marvin's shirt. "What if some crazy homeless guy's in my house?"

"Don't know if it's a good idea, Dad." Danny offered a half-cocked grin. He doubted there was anything to get freaked out about inside. "Maybe Andy should go in first, make sure there aren't any bad guys or boogeymen in there while we wait in the car."

"Funny." Andy uttered a nervous laugh. "Not even on a dare. I hate being alone in *any* house after dark."

"Afraid of the dark?" Danny asked, more serious now.

"No, not the dark—just being *alone* in the dark."

Marvin raised his eyebrows at Danny. "We'll have to take it easy on this one."

"What do you mean?" Andy asked in a high-pitched voice.

"Dad likes to prank my friends when they spend the night," Danny explained quickly. The kid was genuinely freaking out back there. This sort of teasing would have made someone less…troubled laugh. But not Andy. He was serious. "We're always waiting up to see what he'll do next."

"What sort of pranks?"

"Nothing to worry about. Let's get this over with, okay?" Marvin sighed. "We shouldn't keep Ryan waiting."

"You're not sending me in there are you?" Andy asked.

"Not by yourself. I'll go with you."

Andy paused for a moment, thinking. "Okay."

"Hey," Danny said, taking a final stab a humor. "You're not leaving me out here all alone."

They walked up the brick stairs to the front door. Andy said, "Key is under the flower pot, there."

Marvin bent in front of the badly dried plant, rolled it aside, and got the key. Junk mail, flyers, and letters overwhelmed the mailbox mounted beside the door and he gathered them, passing the stack to Danny to hold while he unlocked the door. They stepped into the dark, stale house. Andy held tight to the back of Danny's shirtsleeve, like he feared he might shrug free, run back outside, and slam the door, barricading Andy inside the darkened house.

Andy's free hand slid along the wall and snapped on the light. His voice cracked as he said softly, "Don't scare me please."

They nodded in the oppressive silence. The cold, deep hush of a house abandoned for days overwhelmed them. They moved forward in a little cluster, quietly looking over furniture and tables with about a week's accumulation of dust on their surfaces. Something smelled—growing worse as they neared the kitchen. The odor of garbage forgotten.

Along the hall, photographs of Andy as a younger, happier boy hung on the wall. The eerie silence made the hair along Danny's arm stand up. Not scared in the full meaning of the word, but a sense of lingering doom. Like he had invaded the scene of a crime and the murderer was still there watching him checking out the house of dead people.

Dead people's house...

Andy let go of him and moved more confidently ahead. A sudden crunch and grind beneath their feet stopped Danny and his dad from taking another step. Andy turned back. The shattered remains of a vase littered the hardwood floor below the sideboard.

"Forgot to clean that up. Sorry." Andy flipped lights on

as he went, but instead of bringing the home back to life, it only revealed how very empty the house was and had been standing. If people were really looking for Andy, they weren't checking his house.

Andy turned into that British famous lifestyles host, showing them around as if everything was normal and his mom would walk in the door, arms full of groceries. Somehow, that was worse than him gripping Danny's shirt like a scared little kid on Halloween.

"This is our kitchen, it's kind of small, but it's only me and my mom living here. You can lay the mail on the counter," he said.

Aside from the dust, everything was clean and organized, except for the broken phone in the corner. The shattered plastic, wire guts spewed out on the floor, seemed horrible, ominous.

Without a word, Andy picked up a dirty glass in the sink. Even from where Danny stood, he could see the lipstick imprint of a woman's mouth blurred one edge. Clearly this was the last glass his mom drank from before she died.

Andy explored the smudge as he held it up, eyes glistening with tears. He telegraphed every intense thought and feeling to Danny and his dad on an unmistakable wave of despair. Beneath running water, he rinsed the glass as if washing away his mother, erasing every trace of her.

To comfort him, had she kissed him when he was little and hurt to make the pain go away, maybe kissed him goodnight? Those were all things he used to yearn for when his mom first left when he was little. He couldn't imagine what it must be like to have that your whole life and then it suddenly disappearing. Any envy he might have had for Andy's time with his mother drained away, leaving behind pity.

Water splashed the empty stainless steel sink as Andy stood there, unmoving, unblinking and holding the glass. Danny sent his father a concerned look and he shook his head slightly. Don't interfere, the look said, let him be.

"Sorry," Andy said, his voice thick as if he sensed their unease. "Sorry."

He placed the glass gently, carefully in the dishwasher. His back to the sink, he said, "She never leaves dishes in the sink. Never. She must have been in a hurry."

Marvin cleared his throat, "Andy…"

He blinked and turned, like hiding a secret he had inadvertently given away.

Marvin went to his side and put a hand on his shoulder. "It's all right, son. It's okay."

Andy nodded and used his sleeve to scrub away the tears.

Danny looked at the back door, letting the guy have some privacy while he got himself together. An old-fashioned black answering machine sat beside the phone, the red light blinking. "Hey, you got messages. How do you play them?"

"Just press play."

Danny did. *"Dude this is Jason, where are you, everybody is looking for you, call me…everyone's spazzin' out."*

There was a message from his aunt Lily, she also asked

176

to be called and left a number. Marvin grabbed a pen and wrote it down. There weren't any after that, which was odd, because you'd think once word got out that his mom had died, people would call from all over the place asking about the funeral and stuff. Maybe that was just the movies though, because he'd never actually been to a funeral or around when anyone died like this.

"Hey," Danny said, forcing a cheery tone that sounded forced. "Can I see your room? Help you grab some stuff before we go?"

He nodded and Danny followed him up the stairs, leaving his father sorting through the mail on the counter. Andy's room still looked like he was twelve. Space ships and galaxies covered a blue border around a room filled with everything from sports stuff to Bionicles. An old Styrofoam model of the planets orbited one corner and a poster of a big rig hung behind the door.

Andy went to his closet and tossed a bag onto the bed. On the floor, a broken picture frame lay splintered, but Danny pretended not to notice as he unzipped the bag. "Here, toss me the stuff and I'll pack it in for you."

Andy threw clothing at him first from the closet then from the drawers in the chest on the far wall. The bag filled quickly. "I can't get anything else in here."

"I got another bag under the bed." He dropped to his knees and pulled out a small duffle bag. "I think I lost most of my stuff at the airport. Don't know what I did with it all."

Danny pulled the bag closer to him as Andy started pulling stuff off the shelves and flat surfaces around his room. Odds and ends, like a signed Norfolk Admirals hockey puck, a short soccer trophy, and a few paperback books. "What's all this for?"

Andy shrugged and tossed in a second pair of shoes. He called from the bathroom. "I don't know what's gonna happen to my house." When he came back into the bedroom, he tucked his toothbrush, toothpaste, hairbrush, and deodorant into a side pocket. "I don't want to leave anything behind that's important."

Oh jeez, Danny thought. He hadn't even thought about that. Everything in this guy's life had totally changed. He loses both his parents and his house too. Just didn't seem right. Each of them grabbed a bag and Andy took the pillow from his bed. Danny pretended not to notice that either. The last thing Andy needed was someone to poke fun about his insecurities. They headed down the stairs and into the brightly lit foyer.

Marvin turned the lights off in the kitchen and joined them. He pointed to the bulging duffle bags. "What's all that?"

"It's my stuff," Andy said.

"What stuff?"

"You know, some clean clothes, toothbrush…my stuff," Andy replied with a worried smile.

"Are you moving out?"

"Well, I am spending the night at your house right?"

"Well yeah, *a* night."

"You don't sound sure," Andy asked, raising eyebrows at Danny.

"Dad's just didn't expect you'd bring so much stuff." He turned to his father. "He's just got all his important stuff, since he doesn't know what's gonna happen with the house and everything."

"Okay. But we're going to call your Aunt Lily in the morning, all right?"

Andy tried to hide his disappointment by nodding, but Danny saw it plain as day. No wonder those kids from the beach played him so easy. The guy would totally suck at poker.

They left, turning the lights off inside and the porch light on before locking the door. Marvin opened the trunk and they shoved the duffle bags and pillow inside.

Back in the car, Andy asked, "Is the bowling alley far? Have you been there a lot? Does Ryan have his own ball?"

Danny laughed and answered his questions, casting a glance at his father once in a while. Marvin wore *the look*. He could have told his father not to fight it, because for whatever reason, Andy's visit already felt permanent, like it was supposed to happen or something. His father often talked about how everything happened for a purpose and Danny believed him, especially now.

His dad caught his eye once and smiled reassuringly, as if to say don't worry, he wasn't about to let Andy wander off and lose himself in the streets again, that they would do what they could to help him and keep him safe.

And just like that, Andy dropped into their lives like a snowflake in the summer, unexpected and with no warning or invitation. Danny hoped everything would work out for them all.

CHAPTER 16

Beginner's Luck

Ryan had an alley reserved for them already. After a quick, backslapping hug, Danny introduced Andy.

"Hey man, good to meet you." Ryan grinned and pumped his hand, lightening their moods immediately. He turned to Marvin. "You do know I'm gonna kick your butt tonight, right?"

"I wouldn't bet on it." He laughed. "Let's get our shoes and pick out our bowling balls."

Shy now that Ryan was there, Andy didn't talk much at all. Danny hoped he'd relax more before the night was over. His silence kept everyone casting wary glances and hesitant smiles in his general direction.

"Hey," Ryan said. "Remember what happened to that chick?"

Marvin and Danny burst out laughing.

"That was hilarious!" Danny turned to Andy. "About two years ago, we were at this alley out by Virginia Beach and this woman had way too much to drink. She had this super heavy ball and we watched her fight that thing all night. By the time she could hardly stand, she went to throw the ball, but it didn't come off her fingers. She did a front flip and landed hard on the lane. Her shoe flew off and ended up in the gutter. She wasn't hurt, but man, she could have won

180

America's Funniest Videos on that one."

Andy's chuckle sounded unsure. "Sounds funny."

"It was. Here, I'll help you pick the right kind of ball," Danny said to Ryan. "He's only done this once before so we're gonna have to help him along."

They got everything they needed, including a pitcher of soda and an order of pizza then headed for their lane. Danny sat at the scoreboard table, like always. Ryan had entered their names already and he added Andy's at the end. At Andy's frown, he said, "Sorry dude. Newbie's always have to go last."

Ryan said, "Think of it as a chance to watch and get familiarized with everything again, Andy. You should pick up the game in no time at all."

"Oh, sure," Andy said, testing the weight of his bowling ball. "No problem. I don't mind at all."

Marvin led them off with a spare. Ryan got a gutter ball and cleaned up eight pins on his second throw. Danny took position, lined himself up, and gave the ball a perfect little twist at the end. As soon as it left his fingers, he knew it would be a strike. He waited, watched it pretend to head for the left side gutter, then spin back to center and knock the front pin sideways. It knocked the rest down with a satisfying clatter. "Yes! Ha," he yelled, jumping up. "In your face. I got the first one!"

Ryan pretended to be disappointed, his eyes laughing. "Man, I was robbed. My ball's warped or something."

"Okay, you two, settle down or Andy's gonna think you're both psycho." Marvin marked the strike on the board and smiled at Andy. "You think you got it? Would you like some pointers?"

Andy shook his head. "I think I got it."

Visibly nervous, he slid some as he bent and let go of the ball too soon. The ball landed with a loud thump and slowly twisted down the lane. He watched, jaw dropped like a kid who just threw a rock through a window. Danny wished him some beginners luck. They bowled a lot and he would need some if he planned to keep up. It would totally suck for the kid if he lost every round. The ball impacted just off center. Two pins remained standing, but his ball didn't have enough momentum for the machine to recognize it and they had to push reset at the return.

Eyes almost as big as his bowling ball he asked, "What happened?"

Danny explained and for the rest of the night, as he hoped, Andy did pretty good for a newbie. They stopped for pizza, drinks, and nachos. Andy ate like there was no tomorrow.

Ryan finished his soda. "You should play again with us next weekend. If I can make it back in town one last time before I have to get back to school."

Unaware of the situation, Ryan didn't realize that might be impossible. What would Andy say to him? Would he tell him the truth? Blurt out that he was an orphan like he did in the car? Danny held his breath, hoping Andy could enjoy more before having to get all heavy again.

"If it works out, that would be really awesome." He scooped the last of his cheese up with a nacho.

"Yeah," Danny said, totally relieved that they weren't gonna have to go through the story all over again. He felt for the kid, really did, but Andy needed some fun, not another depressing talk. "We should make plans."

In the second game he held his own against Danny, who lost enthusiasm after he lost to Ryan. He didn't feel too bad though. Andy's beginner's luck kicked into high gear and he ended with a fairly decent score. Watching him joke around with Ryan was better than whining. Besides, he kicked his dad's tail.

Andy sat beside Marvin as they all put their street shoes on again. "Thanks for bringing me."

Danny watched his father's response. Andy couldn't have planned it any better if he'd done it on purpose, and Danny was pretty sure there was nothing calculated in that sincere appreciation on his face.

His dad ate up gratitude like a bear goes after honey. Mostly because it was so rare he heard any.

He smiled and clapped Andy on the back. "My pleasure."

"It was great to meet you, Andy. Hope to see you next weekend." Ryan shouldered his bag and shook the kid's hand again. Then he gave Danny and Marvin a quick wave and headed out the door.

By the time they got home, Danny could hardly keep his eyes open. What a long day, he thought as they pulled into the garage they never finished cleaning. He yawned and followed everyone inside. "Got work in the morning," he said. "Hope you don't mind, but I'm gonna hit the hay."

"Good night," his father called as he draped his jacket on the back of a kitchen chair. "Andy, if you're getting tired, you can crash on the couch."

"Thanks," he said. "Night, Danny."

"Night, Andy."

Upstairs, Danny kicked off his shoes, flopped on the edge of his bed, wriggled off his jeans, and pulled the covers over him. He stretched and sighed, burning eyes staring at the ceiling as he listened to his father setting up the couch for Andy. Their conversation was too low for him to hear, but memories of his dad coming in at night when he was a kid painted the scene in his imagination. He could see his dad tossing the blanket over Andy, asking him if he needed anything or if he wanted a light left on, even if the kid was the same age as Danny.

A few minutes later he heard the sound of his dad's steps coming up the stairs. He closed his eyes and rolled to his side, too tired for any sort of heart-to-heart about Andy. He really didn't want to hear about how the kid wouldn't be able to stay with them. He knew that already, but he'd been raised to worry about people in trouble and couldn't help it. Marvin paused outside the bedroom door. Danny concentrated on breathing deep, trying to sound asleep, even opening his mouth a bit more to give the full effect.

It must have worked because his father resumed his trek to his own bedroom and closed the door. For a while, Danny listened to his dad getting ready for bed and then the squeak of mattress as he settled in for the night. No sounds came from below, but that didn't mean Andy wasn't awake, prowling the downstairs, hunting for expensive items to run off with and try to pawn.

That freckled face glowing with pride the first time he had a strike and the way Ryan instantly liked him made

Danny feel bad about his thoughts. But then again, they said serial killers were often really nice guys when they weren't murdering you. What if Andy decided to just kill them in their sleep so he could take as much time as he wanted searching the house?

Too much imagination, he thought even as he began to drift. When sleep claimed him, the dreams began. Andy lying on the side of the road, covered in blood in a twisted landscape of blackened buildings and broken glass. He tried to shout to the kid to get up, to run before the guy in cowboy boots came back, but Andy couldn't hear him. He tried to run to him, but his legs wouldn't work. No matter how hard he fought, he couldn't help him. Beyond the curled body of the boy, the dark shapes of a kid with a big stick and another with a skateboard passed beneath the red flickering light above a door.

He woke in a sweat, heart thudding loud in his ears. Swinging his legs over the edge of the bed, he rubbed sleep from his face and looked at the clock. Three in the morning. He should be dead asleep. The kid had gotten to him more than he thought.

The hall light was on.

His dad never left it on.

Curious, Danny fumbled to the hallway. Down the stairs, the house lay in shadows, the quiet of no one up or stirring around gave it an empty feel. The other way down the hall, he saw his father's door was open a crack. This was weird, because he normally kept it closed so Danny's alarm wouldn't wake him up, not to mention the light from the hall shining into the darkened room. Definitely something he didn't like.

Danny padded on bare feet down the hall, running a hand along the wall as he kept trying to blink sleep out of his eyes. He listened at the door. A soft snoring noise came from within.

His dad didn't snore.

He pushed the door open slowly, quietly.

Andy lay on the floor at the foot of the bed, the blanket from the back of the couch tangled in his legs, head nestled in the crook of his arm, mouth parted. The soft snores came from him.

Danny stood there, even more confused now that he'd sorted it all out. Why was a guy his age sleeping at the foot of his dad's bed like a…

Like a rescued stray.

CHAPTER 17

Chased by Bad Guys

Danny got home from work and when he walked in, the smell of bacon still lingered in the air. His whole day had been weird, like being in an alternate universe that was so close to the one he lived in, no one would believe him if he said something was off about this world. Andy never was far from his mind, nor was finding him sleeping at the foot of his dad's bed. That was just flat out strange.

By the time eleven a.m. rolled around and his four-hour shift ended, he had developed an oddball theory. Once, there was a kid named Max who lived with them for like two weeks. One of the shortest stays he could remember, and probably would have forgotten about the kid completely if he hadn't turned into his father's shadow.

Though Max was seven, he still sucked his thumb and he wandered in Marvin's footsteps, and if he got left behind, watch out. He flew into these terrible rages. Danny had been about ten then and his dad explained the kid saw him as a replacement for the father he lost. Andy had lost both a mother and a father and he probably wanted a new father.

Well, it wouldn't be the first time Danny had shared his dad with a troubled kid. He used to resent the heck out of that, especially if the foster kid had serious issues that kept Marvin from coming to his practices or games. But, over the years, he learned that he was darned lucky to have a real home and a real dad who cared about him and didn't envy the foster kids anymore.

He sure as heck didn't envy Andy.

Danny found them upstairs in his father's office. "Hey, guys. What's up?"

His father smiled to him, leaning back in his office chair. "Andy was just about to tell me about this dream he had last night."

Andy grinned, his hair still mussed from sleep, but looking well scrubbed and bright eyed. "I had this awesome dream."

Danny leaned in the doorframe, thinking about how un-awesome his own dream had been. "Tell me about it."

"There were these bad guys chasing us, yeah... you were there and those kids who stole your wallet at the flea market. My aunt Lily hired them to find and catch me. They were about to beat me up again, you know, it was where they beat me up in real life, but this time I was running from them, then you came around the corner in the Porsche, with the top down.

"You pulled up beside me, grabbed my arm, and pulled me in the car at full speed, just before they could catch me. But this time I knew you, you weren't a stranger like when I first met you. I was actually hoping you'd come speeding around the corner out of nowhere to save me and you did.

"Then they got into a car, it was one of those old police cars, you know like those big ones, just in a different color and they chased after us, but then suddenly I was at my aunt's house, I looked out of the window and you were doing donuts in the Porsche in front of her house, a huge cloud of smoke coming from your tires. You were waiting for me. I was getting my stuff out of my aunt's house I guess.

"I ran outside and my aunt was after me shouting. '*Come back here Andy!*' She was slower, but she was still right behind me and about to grab my jersey. I couldn't get away from her no matter how fast I ran. You know like when you have a nightmare, somebody is after you, and you run, but don't seem to get away?

"Anyway, I dove into your car, but my aunt got a hold of my foot. When she tried to pull me back my shoe came off and we took off down the street. She stood there with one of my shoes in one hand and her cane in the other.

"Then the bad guys were after us again and my aunt shouted at them as they passed her, '*That way, they went that way. Hurry up you morons.*' The end of her street turned into a highway and all of the sudden there were police cars next to us in the left lane, I don't know if they were trying to catch us or if they were chasing the bad guys.

"The bad guys were in the right lane getting closer, we were in the middle lane and the police almost next to us. We had so much fun outrunning them. I was sitting with my back against the door. Then the bad guys started shooting at our tires. Bang! Bang!" He held up his fingers in the shape of the gun, bending his thumb on each word.

"You slammed on the brakes and one of the bullets hit the right front tire of the police car instead. Man, the tire exploded and the police car flipped over like ten times right in front of us and landed in the right lane. The bad guys couldn't slow down quick enough and ran right into the upside down police car and both cars exploded on impact. It was awesome.

"We laughed and cheered because we were so happy that we got rid of them. As we passed the big fireball you looked at me, but it was weird because I wasn't laughing and cheering anymore like you did. You stopped laughing and looked very concerned like something was wrong with me. Then you asked me. *'What's wrong Andy?'* I pulled my right hand from behind my back and it was full of blood. One of the bullets had gone right through the passenger door and hit me in the back.

"You freaked out and I was just calm and quiet and scared because I was dying and I knew I was dying. There wasn't anything you could do to save me this time, so you got very sad and you kept telling me to hold on until we got to a hospital. Then I died. When I woke up, I checked my back for blood because the dream was so real, but there was none. I was so relieved, but then you weren't sitting on the couch anymore and the TV was off. I got really scared, so I came upstairs and slept in your room."

His father stared, stunned. Danny didn't talk either. He was still trying to get his mind around the kid dreaming about dying and thinking it was an awesome dream. Sounded more like a nightmare to him. He once heard that if you die in your dreams, you die for real. Maybe he meant more like joining his mom in heaven or something, though that wasn't much better.

"Wow," Danny said, recovering. "I think I would have looked for another place to sleep too, if I'd had that dream."

"Next time, wake me up though," Marvin said. "We've

got a roll-away cot you could use. Much more comfortable than the floor."

"I didn't want to bother you," Andy said. "And I was fine. Your carpet is much better than some of the places I've had to sleep recently."

"Speaking of sleeping arrangements," his father said, using a very bad segue. "We should call your aunt."

Danny wished this would have happened while he was at work. Andy could start crying and as bad as he felt for him, tears made him uncomfortable. What do you do when a guy starts to cry?

Marvin set the cordless phone beside Andy. "It's time to call her."

He stared at the phone. "Do I have to?"

Danny wished his dad would call for Andy. The kid looked ready to throw up.

His father handed Andy the slip of paper with the number he'd written down. "She'll be so relieved to hear from you, I'm sure."

He took the paper and lifted the phone with dread sketched across his face.

"Danny and I will give you some privacy, but we won't be far." In the hall, he motioned for Danny to follow him into his room. He left the door slightly ajar so they could hear when Andy finished his phone call.

"What's up?" Danny asked.

"I found this, when we were at his house. I didn't know what to do with it, so I brought it with me." He handed a letter to Danny. "It's from a funeral home."

The thick envelope was addressed to John Henderson

C/O Nancy Riley.

"You think I should to try to get in touch with him? Maybe he's a relative or another family friend who arranged the funeral. I don't think we should open it though."

"I don't know, Dad. Don't you usually have to go through a social worker for this sort of thing? I mean, to make decisions for Andy 'cause he's not eighteen yet?"

His father nodded. "You think I should give the letter to him, then?"

Danny shrugged. "Probably. But if you haven't noticed, he's really broken up."

"I think I'll hold on to this a little while longer. See what his aunt has to say."

Danny thought that was a good plan. Anything to keep more pain from reaching the guy. They went into the hall, each moving quietly so as not to disturb Andy, but wanting to be there for him if he called them back.

Andy said, "Yes… I don't know…not really…I will."

The conversation didn't sound like it would end soon and they headed down the stairs. In the kitchen, they puttered around, cleaning up the breakfast dishes and wiping down the counters. Every now and again, one of them would stop and glance toward the second floor.

About the time Danny thought he had never cleaned so much in his life, a door slammed upstairs and footsteps went to the bathroom. Another door slammed.

"That didn't sound good," Marvin said, draping his washcloth over the sink divider.

"Should we go up?"

"Give him a few minutes. See if he comes down first.

He might just want his privacy."

The next twenty minutes crawled by and Danny felt worse with every second. What if he was up there trying to slit his wrists with his dad's razor or something? He didn't think he'd ever seen a kid so messed up, even with all the fosters that ran through their home. "We should check on him, Dad, don't you think?"

Marvin nodded and led the way up the stairs. He knocked on the bathroom door with one knuckle and asked, "Andy, are you okay?"

Seconds passed, Danny's heart beating heavily as they strained to hear any answer, no matter how muffled or low. His father cocked his head and stared at him.

Finally, so low they wouldn't have caught it if either of them had been breathing louder, Andy said, "I don't know."

Marvin asked, "Can I come in?"

A moment later, he said, "Yes."

Andy sat on the toilet lid, his face red and raw from crying, cradled in his hands. His bangs were wet and stuck up, as if he'd been running tear-slick fingers through the mass over and over again. He made a pitiful picture and the sheer enormity of his anguish left Danny uncertain that he should stand there staring, or if he should let his dad handle it all. He compromised and leaned against the wall in the hallway, still there, still listening, but not staring.

"What happened?" Marvin asked softly.

Andy sniffed and coughed. "I—she—don't..." A sob escaped him and the tears began anew. "My mom's really dead."

The tortured noise he made brought tears to Danny's

eyes and closed his throat on a knot of empathy. He could hardly breathe, that grief so tragically real. He shifted his weight and swallowed hard, holding back his own tears.

"She's dead. Gary's dead. They're all dead!"

The crying grew for a moment, then quieted, muffled and Danny stole a glance into the bathroom.

Marvin hunkered down in front of the boy. Andy buried his face in the crook of his neck, arms wrapped around him, hands in tight fists as the tears flowed from his eyes.

Danny looked at his feet. He'd heard a lot of horrible things, knew there were terrible people in the world. Mother's who chose drugs over their kids; step-dad's who beat their stepchildren, parents in prison for dealing or stealing. None of them, however, seemed as horribly painful right now as what Andy suffered. He wanted to cover his ears and close his eyes before the sound embedded itself on his brain forever.

The sobs finally slowed, then turned to hiccups. "I don't know what to do."

"It's going to be all right, Andy."

Danny wasn't so sure. He'd never heard pain like that before. It had raised the hackles on the back of his neck and left him shaken. He couldn't imagine what it must be like to actually experience those feelings.

"Did you know Gary very well?" Marvin asked softly. "I mean, was he a big part of your life?"

"When my dad died him and his wife helped my mom. They didn't come around for a while then he got divorced and started coming around again. That was a few months ago. I never even liked him. He was like my dad's best friend

194

and… and he wanted to be with my mom. I could never do that."

Water ran in the sink and there was a moment of quiet. When Andy spoke again, he sounded better. "I caught Gary kissing her. I got upset and my mom took his side. She said he was just a friend. A friend doesn't just kiss his best friend's wife, not like that. I think my mom wanted somebody to take care of her. Why she picked Gary, I don't know. She knew I didn't like him."

"If this Gary guy is such a jerk, I wonder why your mom liked him."

"Okay, maybe he's not all that bad, but he used to make fun of me when I was a kid. I used to have this camping chair. I took it with me wherever I went. My dad gave it to me. I wouldn't get rid of it, even after it broke. Only I knew how to use it right."

Danny imagined him running around with a broken chair.

"You know how some kids have that security blanket or suck on a piece of cloth?" Andy asked.

Marvin raised a comical brow. "You mean you liked to suck on a camping chair? Didn't that mess up your teeth?"

Andy's giggle was soft and raw from all the crying. In the hall, Danny smiled, happier to hear that than what had come before.

Marvin said, "So tell me the rest."

"One year, my parents, me and Gary with his wife and his daughter, who was like thirteen or fifteen, went camping. I can't remember. My dad forgot to call the place and reserve a spot for us. When we got there, nobody was allowed to camp in that park because of this big concert going on. We ended up leaving and Gary got pretty mad at my dad. We went to Gary's house because it was closer."

Danny leaned around the corner and smiled encouragingly into the reddest, puffiest eyes he'd ever seen on anyone. "What happened there?"

Andy's smile faltered. "I had to share a room with his daughter who was ticked off at me I guess, or mad because we didn't get to go camping. She had a real bad attitude and fought with her dad. He tried to cheer her up, but she wanted me to sleep somewhere else because of the camping chair thing. He got mean, said I was weird and took my chair and pretended to sit on it. They laughed, thought it was so funny. I got so mad I started crying like crazy. He tried to calm me down before my dad heard, said it was just a joke. I hated him after that."

Happy to have the subject off Andy's mother, Danny asked, "Did you end up staying there sharing a room with his daughter?"

"No. We left and went to that concert. I remember in the parking lot after, it was so crowded. These two old ladies had a car so stuffed they had a bag hanging from a coat hanger jammed in the window. When they turned right in front of me, the bag swung out and I had to leap out of the way to avoid being murderized in a drive-by bagging."

They all laughed and their voices bounced on the tiles in the bathroom, amplifying their need to move past Andy's pain, louder than genuine amusement. Whatever the real story was, if it wasn't what Andy had told them, Danny didn't really care. He had no doubt the kid was in deep and needed all the help he and his dad could give. Every bit of it.

CHAPTER 18

Clearing Cobwebs

"Well what do you say?" Marvin asked, stretching in the sunshine as he stood in the middle of the driveway. "Let's get this garage cleaned out for real this time, hey?"

Andy said, "Sure. Anything I can do."

Danny shrugged. He'd already been to work that morning, not like he wanted to spend the afternoon to doing more. But, his dad was determined and Andy was eager. He just wasn't the sort of guy who could sit around and watch everyone else work.

Marvin pulled a bunch of bags out of a large box and tossed it into the center of the floor. "Anything we want to get rid of, toss in there and once that's filled, we can start using the bags. I'll make a trip to the thrift store when we're done and donate it all so make sure it's not broken. Anything that is broken goes in the trash."

The garage felt like a sauna and the loft was simply unbearable. Danny wished it would be enough to take his mind off the phone call Andy made to his aunt. Whatever was said during that call must have been horrible. He kept imagining what it could have been. Maybe she blamed Andy? That would have been the worst.

Sweat poured off him as he blackened his hands digging through rubber gaskets, oiled car parts, and hoses of every shape and size. Every drop that fell from his forehead, turning the grime to sludge, counting each moment his curiosity wasn't satisfied. Danny kept his mouth shut, afraid to say the wrong thing and set the kid off again, but Andy didn't stop talking. Not to complain, though. Any one of his buddies from school or work would have been crabbin' up a storm by now.

Andy couldn't stop asking questions. "What's this go to?"

"It's a timing belt." Marvin pointed to a bag full of belts. "You can put it in there."

"What's a timing belt do?" Andy asked.

"Keeps the internal moving engine parts in order."

"And what does this do?"

"That's a new line for the weed eater. We're putting yard stuff over there."

"Do you have a lot of weeds around here? Hey," Andy said, grabbing the hedge trimmers. "What do you use these for?"

"Keeps the bushes even," Marvin answered.

And so it went, the whole time they worked. Danny's silence wasn't even noticed. His father's patience could have put a monk to shame. A half hour into the constant questioning, Danny thought he would explode.

But then Andy slipped in a question that Danny really wanted to know the answer to as well. "Do you think I can stay here for a while?"

Marvin tripped over the garden hose he was winding and tried to brace himself by grabbing the end of a rake. Missing by a fraction, he spun hard to avoid a painful landing on the gas grill. His heel hit the rake, which caused the long wooden handle to smack him soundly in the rear. Propelled forward into a column of old tires he caught himself just before his nose slammed into the hard rubber. Bent oddly on all fours, he looked like a bad mime trying to be an elephant.

Danny let out a hoot and guffawed so hard he could barely breathe.

Andy covered his mouth with both hands, trying to be more polite about his own laughter.

"Oh, man." Andy gasped, grinning. "You okay?"

Red faced, Marvin straightened and wiped his hands on his jeans. "Yeah. I'm fine."

Danny caught enough of his breath to say, "Dad, that rake just kicked your butt!"

"Yeah, yeah," Marvin said, waving toward them holding their bellies and wobbling as they cackled. "I'm sure it was hilarious. But let's get this done, okay?"

A full five minutes passed until they could completely stop laughing. Danny took the shop broom and started pushing dirt toward the open end of the driveway, wishing he'd thought fast enough to snap a shot of it all with his cell phone.

Behind him, Andy asked, "So is it okay for me to stay here?"

Danny hesitated, then started sweeping again, slower so he could hear his father's response.

"Well, I'm not sure," Marvin answered slowly. "What did your aunt say?"

"She didn't really care," Andy mumbled.

"I'd have to talk to her first."

"But if she says it's okay, it's okay with you?" Andy asked.

Danny stopped and leaned on the broom handle, meeting his dad's questioning gaze with a nod. Yeah, it would be good to have another guy in the house. They'd been pretty much on their own for a few years now. Besides, he wanted Andy to be okay.

"If she says it's okay, you can stay for a while if you like."

Andy's eyes shimmered like those of a cat's catching light at night. "For real, you don't mind?"

Marvin nodded.

"I'll help you clean out the guest room," Danny said, preferring the air-conditioned interior to the muggy garage any day.

"That's awesome. I guess we have to go back and get all my stuff. You wanna buy another house? My aunt said they're selling mine."

"Wow." Danny hadn't seen that one coming, though with both of his parents gone and Andy not yet eighteen, it made sense.

"Uh," Marvin said. "I wasn't thinking of moving, but we can get your things."

"Cool. I barely know my aunt anyway. She never married or had any kids or nothing. Far as I know, she barely knew I existed."

Danny asked, "Is she the only relative you have?"

"I got a grandpa I never met…well I did, but I didn't know he was my grandpa. He's my mom's dad and he's… I guess a bum?" Andy explained, "You know somebody who is homeless and lives on the street?"

"Yes. Where did you see him?" Marvin asked.

"At the airport sleeping on a bench. I didn't know he was my grandpa, or that he was there to pick me up. Aunt Lily told me how he got drunk and lost two fingers on his hand, so it had to be that guy. I 'spose I should have felt sorry for him but I was kind of jealous, y'know?"

"Jealous of a guy you thought was a bum?" Danny had second thoughts about letting someone obviously a few gears shy of a full transmission stay with them. "What for?"

"You'll think it's weird." Andy tied the bag of trash closed at the top, not looking at them as he said, "I thought even he had somebody waiting for him and no one could be bothered to pick me up. Funny that he was there for me. I feel really stupid now. But I got you guys so it all worked out."

Before Andy could get all sappy and start hugging them, Danny asked, "You want to see some pictures?"

"That'd be cool." Andy looked at Marvin. "If that's okay."

Marvin gave the garage a good once over and nodded. "We've done enough. And there aren't any rakes in the house."

They grinned at each other and Danny led the way inside. All of them took turns at the sink, washing off and chugging cold water from the dispenser in the fridge.

Marvin said, "I'm gonna grab a shower. Don't throw any wild parties while I'm gone."

Danny cocked a grin at Andy. "You start calling

everyone, I'll order the pizza."

Andy's eyes grew wide and he cast a sidelong glance at Marvin, as if to say Danny was crazy, his dad could still hear him.

"I'm just jokin' with you," Danny said and elbowed him as his dad headed up the stairs. "I'll get the photos. Pop us open a couple of Cokes, okay?"

Danny grabbed a shoebox stored in the back of the closet. They sat at the table and flipped through the pictures until they hit the section full of all the cars his dad had owned over the years.

Impressed, Andy asked, "Wow. Those were all his?"

Danny nodded. "Have you ever driven a car?"

He got quiet. "Not a car, but a semi truck sitting on my father's lap. I guess that doesn't count?"

"You want me to show you how? We can't use the Porsche but we can use my car. I'll ask Dad if it's okay when he gets out."

More relaxed, Danny thought Andy wasn't really all that messed up. Right then, he was just like any one of his buddies. They talked about first-person shooters vs. co-play. Andy liked first person, Danny liked hooking up with other players online. By the time his father came down the stairs, hair wet and smelling like Zest soap, they had gone all the way back to the first Zelda game on the clunky first Gameboys.

"Hey, Dad," Danny said, tilting his chair back on two legs and leaning around Andy to see his father where he stood holding the fridge open. "I was telling Andy I could teach him to drive while he's here. Make it easier on him to get a license later on."

Not exactly the sort of thing Marvin would automatically agree to, Danny was surprised when he did. "Sure. Sounds like a great idea. But I'll have to teach him."

"Really?" Andy spun in his chair. "When?"

"How about now?"

Andy was in the garage before the refrigerator door closed. Danny laughed and got up. No way was he gonna miss this.

They took his station wagon. He hoped his dad would notice what a junker and embarrassment the station wagon really was; it would make his arguments to be handed down the Porsche later all the more reasonable.

Andy started to get into the passenger seat. Marvin said, "First lesson: the driver sits behind the wheel."

"Oh yeah, right." He blushed and detoured around the nose of the car.

Danny got into the back, grimacing at the food wrappers and soda cans he'd forgotten to throw away and hoping his dad wouldn't see the mess. While Marvin buckled into the front passenger seat, he scooped as much of the litter together as he could and tucked it under the seat with his toe. He'd get to it later.

His father said, "We'll take the station wagon around the neighborhood and I'll sit in the passenger seat with my hands on the emergency brake, just in case."

"I don't wanna wreck your car. Are you sure?"

Danny said, "It'll be all right."

"We're starting off slow," Marvin added.

"Okay. If you're okay with it." He latched the seatbelt.

"What do I do now?"

"Start the engine."

Danny remembered that sunny day when he was fifteen and his dad taught him. It didn't seem like it was all that long ago, but he'd already been driving on his own now for two years. Compared to the unsure way Andy gripped the steering wheel, Danny had been ready for NASCAR.

Marvin spoke in a low, soothing voice, an echo of the tone he'd used on Danny. "Keep your foot on the brake and put it in drive."

He did. "Like that?"

"Yes. Now, ease off the brake and slowly, *slowly*, press the accelerator."

He gave it a bit too much gas, then slammed on the brakes, jerking them all forward in their seats. "Sorry!"

"I did that all the time," Danny lied. Maybe once or twice, but that was it. Andy didn't need to know that though.

"It's okay, just take it easy, and try again." Marvin smiled to reassure him and the second time out he got it just right.

He took to driving far easier than Danny expected. Only freaking a couple times when he looked down at his feet to see the pedals instead of keeping his eye on the road. Thankfully, the street was empty at this time on a Sunday.

By the time they pulled back into the driveway, Andy glowed so bright, he was practically neon. He sat straighter, and could have passed for any normal guy getting lessons from his dad—big brother riding in the back for kicks. Danny missed his own mom now and again, but more than anything, he'd missed having someone just to hang out with in the house. Sort of cool again, to have someone around.

CHAPTER 19

The Night it Rained

The whole next week, when Danny didn't have to work, he took Andy around to meet his friends. Because his father owned a dealership, they spent most of the day together. Danny didn't mind, it kept his father busy with someone else's business other than his. When he'd walk in the door, he'd often find them drinking coffee (how Andy could stand the stuff Danny didn't know) in the computer room, now turned into a spare room for Andy.

Unlike most of the guys that had slid through their home, Andy felt like he had always been there and would never leave. Underneath it all, though, was a strange sort of tension, like waiting for the other shoe to fall, but not really believing that other shoe existed at all. If Andy still grieved for his mom, he kept it to himself.

Danny climbed the stairs, bone weary after covering his friend's shift so he could go see Kid Rock in concert. His legs ached and all he wanted was bed. As he trudged down the hall, their easy laughter irritated him. Normally he thought it was cool they got along so well, but tonight, he was cranky. He wanted to be the one in there chillin' with his dad, shootin' the breeze, goofin' around on the computer, maybe playing a game or something.

"Hey, Danny," his father called. "Come in here a sec,

would ya?"

He turned with a heavy sigh and leaned against the doorframe. "What?"

His dad's smile faltered some, but he said, "We were thinking of hitting the bowling alley again tonight. What do you think?"

"I think I'm too tired." Danny didn't mean to sound like a complete jerk, but it irked him that they didn't have to work so hard. "But if you two want to go without me, go ahead."

"Wouldn't be the same without you," Andy said. "Figured you'd want to have some fun after working so much."

Okay, so now he felt like a real heel. "Sorry. I'm just bushed. I'll take a rain check."

He went back to his room and flopped on his bed, toeing one sneaker off after another and then laying there too tired from the effort to do much more than stare out the window.

A full moon cast windowpane squares across his bed. So perfectly round and big, its light cool, calm, and peaceful. He didn't sleep well during a full moon though; the light kept him awake, and sometimes it would wake him from a dead sleep at odd hours. He grabbed a fistful of blanket and rolled to his side, back to the window, and closed his eyes.

At two a.m. something woke him. Clouds advanced on the moon like battleships ready to wage war with rain and thunder, wind and storm. They replaced the magical glow with lightning and mayhem. Thunder rumbled far off. Danny drifted on the edge of sleep. Rain drummed the window.

Somewhere near by a car door slammed.

The familiar crank of a car engine startled him upright, then out of bed. Through the window, in the driveway below, he noticed his station wagon sat idling in the driveway. As he watched, it backed out, rear wheels catching a good chunk of grass before turning toward the road.

A knock came on his door and then his dad stuck his head in the room. "Danny, I think someone's stealing you car."

"Where's Andy?" Danny didn't know why he asked, but he had a bad feeling.

"I don't know."

They both hurried into the hall and to the guest room. Andy was not in his bed. A frightening reality sank in. He had really stolen his car. "Hope you're happy now. You taught him how to drive. I can't believe I ever trusted him."

"That's not helpful," Marvin scolded. "Any idea where he's going?"

"How should I know? You're the one who's all chummy with him."

"Danny, come on. We need to stop him before anything bad happens."

"You're right, I'm sorry." Danny shoved his feet back into his sneakers as his father ran down the hall, shrugging out of his robe.

"Meet you in the Porsche," Marvin called.

He ran down the stairs and into the garage. The cover on the Porsche was gone and the garage door stood open, the rain spraying all the stuff piled near the entrance. He got in just as his dad banged out the door and into the garage.

Marvin slid behind the wheel and turned the ignition, backing out with a harsh squeal of tires that would leave black streaks for the rest of the years they lived there.

"The garage door was already open and the cover gone. You think he was trying to take the Porsche?" Danny asked.

"I don't know, doubt it, it's a stick shift." He glanced at Danny quickly then turned his attention to the rain-slicked road. "Andy won't get far. He doesn't really know how to drive yet and this rain won't make it any easier."

The wind and rain picked up and Danny wondered how his dad could see through the deluge and fog creeping up the window. Marvin twisted the knob to high and the vents began to blow. Did Andy even know how to turn on the wipers or vent to keep the windshield clear? "He's gotta be freaking out, Dad. We have to find him."

His anger was gone now, replaced by an unexpected fear that Andy could really hurt himself out there. Almost a panic.

Grim faced, his father sped down empty streets, both of them tossing out ideas about where he might have gone. Back to Virginia Beach? Not likely. To his house? Maybe, but he was freaked about going there before and they'd already gotten most of his stuff out.

Confused, Danny asked, "Do you think he didn't like it at our house anymore?"

"I don't know. If he wanted to leave, all he had to do was say so. Wait, what's that?"

Up ahead, when the wipers allowed, Danny could see red lights fishtailing on the road, the brake lights coming on for no reason, then the car shooting forward again. He strained against his seatbelt, trying to see through the pouring rain. As their headlights flashed on the back bumper, he recognized his own station wagon immediately. "It's him! Oh, jeez, I hope he doesn't crash. Look at him."

"Let's catch up to him. Maybe you can get him to pull over." Marvin flashed the high beams three times.

He either didn't see it, or didn't know what it meant. The wagon dangerously swerved back and forth between the curb and the centerline, bouncing like a rubber ball.

Clutching the car door, Danny asked, "The wagon's got air bags right? I can't remember."

"I think so." Marvin sped up as the wagon darted ahead. "I hope so."

The traffic light ahead turned yellow, but he didn't stop. He barely made it through the intersection before cars started crossing.

"Keep going! Just run through the red light," Danny urged, but fell silent when a police car drove through the intersection. His father stopped and they watched helplessly as the wagon disappeared. Marvin cursed and hit the steering wheel with the palm of his hand. "Damn!"

"Look." Danny pointed as the station wagon turned far up ahead. "He's not heading to his house. That's the wrong way."

The light turned green and they sped forward. "I think I know where he's going."

"Where?"

"The cemetery."

"Why would he be going to the cemetery in the middle of the night in the pouring rain?" Danny asked.

"A hunch. Worth a try."

Danny kept his fingers crossed they would find him there safe and sound. "If he was having a bad time, why didn't he wake one of us up?"

"I don't know. He's not doing as well as you think. Around you, he's been like normal, like your friends. But around me, he opens up more. He's still got a lot of guilt and it's driving him crazy."

"He should know he can talk to me." Danny didn't understand why it hurt him that Andy didn't trust him enough to open up to him, but it did. Ryan was about the only real family he had, as the other boys had all moved on, and many of them out of state, some of them in prison, unfortunately. He thought of Andy as a kid brother almost, even if they were the same age.

The side streets were darker, the trees whipping violently in the wind that shoved at the Porsche, trying to push it into the oncoming traffic lane. They reached the entrance to the cemetery and caught the taillights of the wagon as it wove along the winding access road. Andy drove much, much too fast for the conditions and Danny's jaw ached from clenching his teeth in anticipation of the crash.

When they rounded the corner, the wagon had gone off the road and gotten stuck in the mud, the driver's door and tailgate wide open. Andy had abandoned the vehicle. No sign of him anywhere.

Marvin eased forward at an angle, using the headlights to sweep the area.

"Where is his mom buried?" They should have brought

him there sooner, Danny thought. Maybe he wouldn't have freaked so much then.

"There!" Marvin pointed. "Over there. I see him."

A darker shadow amongst the drenched dark shapes of the markers moved and Danny saw him too. Barely visible and a good deal away from the wagon, he must have had to hunt for his mother's grave. His father parked the car and Danny opened his door before his dad had his seatbelt off.

Heavy winds blasted rain into his face and he tucked his chin in, squinting to protect his eyes. His dad joined him, splashing through freezing puddle after puddle. By the time they reached Andy, they were soaked.

"Andy," Danny yelled.

He glanced at them, barely registering they were there before renewing his frantic attempts to spread the Porsche cover over the mud and dirt in front of him.

Hair plastered to his head, he screamed desperately, "I can't keep it down! Help me! Hurry up! Please! Help me."

"What are you doing?" Danny shouted, bending for one corner flapping in the wind. Lightening struck on the other side of the neighborhood with a crackle followed by a thunderous roar that swallowed up Andy's pleas.

Marvin bent to help with the tarp. "What are you trying to do?"

"Help me. Just please…help me," Andy yelled hoarsely.

They tried, but the wind blew the cover violently, the slick, hard material slapping them when one of them lost their grip. If he wanted to keep the rain off his mom's grave, he was too late. The soil beneath their feet hadn't had time to get packed down and they sunk in, mud oozing up their ankles and into their shoes.

"She hated the rain," Andy wailed, "She's probably drowning in there. I promised I'd take care of her! I promised!"

Marvin approached him slowly, putting an arm around his thin, soaked shoulders. "The water can't get through to her. She's perfectly safe."

"I don't believe you," Andy screamed and flung off his arm, slapping wildly and aimlessly at him. "She's drowning in there and you won't do anything to help! I hate you!"

"It's the truth," Danny shouted through the rain, "The casket is airtight. That's why magicians use them!"

Andy paused, confused and defeated. "Really?"

"Danny's right, Andy. She's safe and dry. Not a drop of rain can touch her."

Andy covered his face, and slumped. "She hated rain," he whispered, exhaustion wrought in every word. "She hated the rain so much."

"She won't have to put up with rain anymore. She's in a better place," Marvin said as Andy buried his face in his shirt, wadding the fabric in his fists as he sobbed and sobbed.

Danny patted him carefully on the shoulder. No foolin' Andy wasn't over his mom's death yet. He'd hidden it well from him and his friends.

"Let's go home, Andy, and dry off before you get seriously sick, okay?" He glanced up at Danny. "Take him in the wagon. I'll rock you guys out of the mud."

Danny nodded and held a hand out for Andy. He took it and stood, hunched and dejected as he walked barefoot back to the car. He apologized profusely for dragging mud into the station wagon. "I ruin everything."

"Don't worry about it. I still got trash shoved under the seats." Danny tried to smile, but it soured quickly, feeling out of place as the kid beside him bent at the waist and covered his head, like a passenger in a plane getting ready to kiss himself goodbye.

Danny was thankful for the rain. He couldn't tell if he cried or not, but he sure as hell felt bad enough for Andy. His father slapped the hood of the car and nodded. Danny threw the vehicle in reverse and revved the engine. They rocked for a heartbeat, then flew back onto the access road. Apparently, it wasn't stuck as bad as they had thought.

Alone with Andy on the drive home, a drive made even slower by the weather, Danny struggled to think of something, anything to say. Every now and again, a sad mewing would emit from Andy and he'd shift, press his face to the window, and cover his mouth. He needed someone to talk to, a professional. Danny could be his friend, but he couldn't help him in the way he really needed help.

"If you ever want to, like go back there, maybe, again," Danny said. "Just ask. I'll take you."

"I was just borrowing the car. I was gonna bring it back." The words were flat, emotionless with an eerie desolation.

"Okay," Danny said. "I know that's what you meant to do. I just…well I guess this is goofy, but I don't want to see anything bad happen to you, y'know?"

Andy didn't respond and Danny kept silent the rest of the way home. What did a friend do for someone like that? Covered in mud and drenched were the least that was wrong with him, and it was all Danny knew how to help with.

When they got to the house, he pulled into the garage, making sure there was enough room for the Porsche when his dad got there. He got out, but Andy just sat there. He couldn't just leave the guy in the car all night. Danny walked around the car, squeezing between the lawnmower and the hood to get there, and opened the door. His flannel shirt felt tough and wet in his hand as he tugged the kid out of the car. "C'mon," he said, "Let's get you in the house."

They had just stepped onto the mat in front of the door when his father pulled in. Marvin didn't waste time coming to help. He said, "Let's get you into a hot shower and get that mud off you. You'll feel better."

Like a wind-up kid without a key, he let Danny and his father steer him into the downstairs bathroom. Danny got the water running, while his dad made sure Andy understood he was supposed to get in the shower and clean off.

Danny said, "I'll get you some dry jams."

He took the steps wearily to the upstairs bathroom where he cleaned up in the sink and put on fresh clothing. Hair wet, an occasional trickle of water making it down his neck, he went to the guest room to get Andy's clothes. He found his father in there, standing by the bed, holding the clothes and staring into space.

"What's up, Dad?" Danny asked.

He came to life and said, "Nothing. I just wonder if it's a good idea to keep him here. In a way, we're letting him avoid dealing with all this. It's like a vacation from his life. He's got to do something with all that mess inside him before it starts coming out in even more dangerous ways."

"More dangerous?"

He shrugged. "Remember Jorge?"

Danny did. The boy stopped talking and eating after he came back from a visitation with his father. After that, there were no more visits with the boy's natural parents. They had to hospitalize him and feed him intravenously to keep him from starving to death. "Do you really think Andy's that bad off?"

"No. Not…now." He held up the clothes. "I've got this. Get some sleep and we'll talk about this in the morning. Okay?"

Danny nodded and returned to his room, head spinning. He'd looked up the word insane in the dictionary once, wondering what it must be like not to trust your own brain, especially after some of the kids they knew. The definition said something about having no common sense, acting stupid, or being sick in the head. Was Andy going nuts right in front of them?

He lay awake, trying to relax enough to sleep, but his mind raced. Andy had been stupid, running out there and not using his common sense. But then, he could be like sick in the head with grief. Temporary insanity?

Sleep came slowly, creeping up on him for an hour or more. When the floorboards stopped creaking, when springs and doors were closed and he could tell everyone was in bed, he finally decided that he didn't need to know if Andy was crazy. He knew the kid missed his mom and Danny knew what that felt like.

Danny and his dad were eating cereal at the kitchen

table when Andy came down the stairs. Cheeks pink and sounding contrite, he said, "I understand that you're mad at me. That was stupid to take the car. I'm sorry."

"We're not mad at you. We're worried about you." Marvin took a sip of his coffee. "You could have caused a serious accident, possibly killed innocent people, or hurt yourself. You need to think about these things. The car could have been replaced, no big deal, but what if you got hurt really bad?"

Danny said, "Really, we will take you if you want to go."

Andy stared at his shaking hands. "I'm sorry. I should have come to you first, but...I was afraid you guys would be mad if I woke you up."

"Was I ever mad at you?" Marvin asked.

Andy shook his head and sneezed.

Danny asked, "Are you okay?"

Andy nodded.

"Well, that's settled," Marvin asked him, "Hungry?"

"Starving!" Andy sat in front of the empty bowl they'd put on the table for him.

Danny smiled.

Two weeks passed, things running fairly smooth. Every Sunday, Danny's dad talked with Andy's aunt, who didn't seem to be in a hurry to get him up to Baltimore, which was just fine with Danny. He'd even talked to his boss about maybe letting Andy work there for a while. Now all he had to do was find out if Andy wanted to be that far away from Danny's dad for part of the day.

Not jealous as much as just feeling left out. His dad and Andy shared inside jokes at the table and though they often filled Danny in on what was so funny, he never really found anything quite as funny. He was carrying the phone to the living room, thinking of calling the guys over to hang out that weekend when it rang in his hand.

"Hello?"

"I want to speak with my nephew, Andy Riley, please." Though she said please, it wasn't really a request.

"He's not here," Danny said. "He and my dad ran to the video store. They should be back in about half an hour."

"I don't know how long you intend to keep Andy there, but he said he wants to stay the entire summer with you." A dog yipped in the background.

"I don't know. I'm sure it wouldn't be a problem. You'd have to talk to my dad about that though."

"I had hoped to get him settled before school started. But, I suppose we can take care of that later." She sighed.

What was she talking about? "Do you want my dad to call you when he gets home?"

"No. He already told me you're going to Greece or something at the end of the summer."

"Europe," Danny corrected. His dad had lots of family over there and they went once a year to hang out. He loved going.

"Whatever. Andy can stay there until then. Just tell him that he can't expect any money from me. If he's going to keep my nephew there, he's gonna have to support him without anything from me."

The phone went dead. Danny stared at it in disbelief.

That was Aunt Lily? Holy cow, he wouldn't wish her on his worst enemy, let alone Andy. God, the kid had no luck at all. He might as well be facing military camp or one of those cannibal hillbilly types from the horror flicks. He shuddered and set the phone aside, not really feeling up to hanging out with anyone before he could talk to his dad and Andy.

When they walked through the door, laughing about one of their goofy inside jokes again, Danny stood up. He waited nervously, shifting from foot to foot, not sure how he was supposed to tell his dad that Aunt Lily pretty much decided for them that Andy would stay, and whether or not his father would be upset she hadn't talked to him herself.

"Dad, Andy's aunt called." Danny told them what she had said. "Just until we leave for Europe."

Andy's face fell; the laughter drained from his face like someone had opened a spigot in his chest and let him run dry.

Marvin smiled and clapped Andy on the back. "See, told you she'd probably let you stay. This is good news."

"Yeah," Andy said. "Until you guys got halfway around the world and leave me behind."

Danny winced. He would never trade the trip to go live with that woman and her yipping dog. "Could he come with us?"

"Could I?" Hope lit his eyes briefly, then fled when Marvin shook his head.

"It'll be next to impossible to arrange anything now. You don't have a passport and that by itself takes too long, not to mention your aunt would have to arrange for one and I don't think she'd allow you to go." At his sullen expression, he said, "You'll be eighteen soon. Then you can do what you want. Maybe even come stay here for a while, figure out where you want to go to college."

The disappointment on his face softened. "That would be really cool."

"Very," Danny said. "We could look for an apartment together too."

"Awesome," Andy said, grinning again.

"It's settled then. You'll live with your aunt until you turn eighteen. When we get back, I'll call you and let you know we're home again. Then it's just a matter of waiting for your birthday."

Danny thought it was all settled, but as the days past, Andy just wouldn't let it go. Every chance he had, he brought up the trip and some crazy solution, including putting him in a suitcase to smuggle him out of the country, anything so he could go along with them to Europe. Some of his ideas were straight off the Cartoon Network. Though he'd been through a lot, Danny thought, the kid had been totally too sheltered.

Considering his alternative was living with Aunt Lily, Danny didn't blame him. About the time his friends started calling and asking why Andy couldn't go along, though, he got aggravated and tried to remember his father's exceptional patience. He counted to ten a lot.

"It's not the end of the world. We're only four hours away by car and we'll come visit you when we get back." Danny told him one sunny afternoon on the deck. "Let's not ruin the rest of your time with us."

"Yeah," he said, hands tucked deep in his pockets.

"You're right. It's just hard."

Finally, Danny thought. His relief was short lived. Every time mention of the trip came up, Andy froze and grew quiet, withdrawn. The closer they got to the day of their flight, the worse he fell apart. A sick feeling wound inside his gut and he wished he'd been a ton nicer to the kid before he'd given up trying to go.

CHAPTER 20

Saying Goodbye

Danny wanted to be sick. Three weeks had never gone by so fast in his whole life. Every time he got excited about leaving for Frankfurt, his heart plummeted at Andy's disappointment over being left behind. Up and down, up and down, like a landlubber on the high seas, his gut didn't know what to do.

This morning they would take Andy to the train station and send him off to Baltimore to live with an old battle-ax and her little yippy dog. Danny didn't want him to go so he couldn't imagine how badly Andy didn't want to get on the train.

"You almost ready, kiddo?" Marvin asked from the hall.

Danny turned from where he stood beside his bed, adding more stuff to his travel bag that he didn't want to forget. His dad stood in the hall outside the guestroom he now thought of as Andy's room. No answer came from inside.

His father caught his look and shook his head, conveying that he hadn't the foggiest idea how to help. To Andy, he said, "We've only got a few hours. Let's not spend them not talking to each other, okay?"

He opened the door. "You're right. I'm sorry. This just so totally sucks. I wish I could just stow away or something."

"I know." Marvin straightened from the doorframe. "I'll see you downstairs in a few minutes, okay?"

"Yeah. But hey," Andy said, calling him back. "Is it okay if I leave some of my stuff here? I mean, if I'm coming back and all?"

Marvin nodded. "We'll keep it safe for you until you get back."

His father went down the stairs and Danny turned his attention back to the assorted Nintendo DS games he wanted to bring. About the time he'd double-checked to see that everything was there, Andy emerged from his room. He dragged a suitcase and two duffle bags that were slung over his shoulders.

Danny caught up to him at the top of the stairs. He grasped the back of one bag and said, "Here, I'll help."

Maybe he had surprised Andy, or overbalanced him or something, he didn't really see, but he fell forward, missed the railing, and tumbled to the bottom in a ball of flailing limbs and luggage. The suitcase landed on his belly and he let out a woof of air.

"Oh man." Danny ran down after him. "Dude, are you okay? Dad!"

Marvin rushed in from the garage. "What happened?"

"He fell down the stairs," Danny explained.

"My fault," Andy said, "Should have been more careful. Tried to carry too much."

"Can you stand up?" Marvin asked.

"I can't get up, you need to help me. I think I broke my leg. I can't go on a train like this."

Grabbing his arms, they helped pull him up. He stood on his right leg and hopped with assistance to the sofa. "I think I need to go to the doctor. This is pretty serious. My leg hurts like it's broken."

"Did you ever break a bone before?" Marvin knelt and elevated his leg.

He hissed in pain. "No, that's why I'm thinking it's broke. We need to see a doctor and it's probably a good idea to call my aunt and tell her what happened."

Danny hovered, not sure what to do, feeling responsible, until his dad rolled up Andy's pants leg. It looked totally normal. Not a thing wrong with it. His dad met his gaze, reflecting his own skepticism.

His father asked Andy, "Can you move your toes?"

He did, but barely, grimacing in exaggerated pain.

"I think you'll be fine." He stood. "It's probably just bruised."

"Okay," he said, dejected, but he limped until they left the house.

Once the bags were packed in the trunk and they started for the station, time slowed to a horrible crawl and moved equally too fast. Waiting to say goodbye felt like torture, but it was taking them forever to get there and Danny could hardly sit still. Andy didn't talk at all, just stared out the window, arms crossed, forehead resting on the glass.

His dad kept trying to start light-hearted chatter, but no one responded and he finally gave up all together. Danny felt like a traitor. Here he'd talked his dad into letting Andy stay, each week pointing out how great it was to have him around, and this time, he couldn't do a thing. He'd even checked online and his dad had been right about the passport thing. Especially for a minor. It totally sucked.

At the station, Andy didn't even take his bags out of the trunk. He just walked ahead and stood outside the station doors.

"I can't think of leaving him alone, Dad. What's gonna happen to him? Without us, I mean?" He whispered, taking the luggage out slow enough to buy time for his response.

"He'll be fine. Aunt Lily might never win Miss Congeniality, but it's only for a few weeks and then he can come back."

Danny nodded. He was right, of course, but that didn't make him feel any less guilty. If he had ever met anyone less capable of taking care of himself, Danny didn't know it. Sure, Andy pitched in around the house, even made Danny look like a total slacker, but if it came down to making any kind of common sense or important decision, forget it.

"He'll be okay. Now come on, before he misses his train." His dad spoke softly, kindly as he dragged Andy's suitcase behind him and shouldered one of the bags.

Danny nodded and took the last bag, closing the trunk with a thud of finality. *Here we go.* He took a deep breath and tried to smile. It helped that Andy had given up the fake limp completely.

Inside the station, they checked his suitcase and got his ticket. They stood together uncomfortably. Danny had the sense that Andy didn't really want him there. Not because he didn't want to say goodbye to him, but because he wanted to be alone for a minute with Marvin.

"Think I'll use the restroom. Be right back," Danny said,

walking away and having absolutely no need for a bathroom. He meandered in the general direction, killing a few minutes and giving them time together. He'd seen this before, even gotten punched once by one of the foster kids. They wanted Danny's dad for their own and saw him not as much as a threat—just competition. Which was crazy, if anyone thought about it. There were tons of families who had lots of kids and the parents had enough love for them all.

He rounded a soda machine and leaned back to watch. His dad held Andy in his arms, the boys hands fisted in the back of Marvin's coat. The moment lingered, people trying not to watch, but doing so anyway. He was glad now, that he hadn't invited along some of his friends to see Andy off, to try to make it a party.

His father pulled back, clapping Andy on the shoulder twice and saying something that made the kid nod.

Danny waited another two minutes then headed back, walking slow and giving them time to see him before he got too near. He prayed Andy wouldn't hug him like that, make him all teary eyed. He was too old to cry like a baby over going on a vacation. Any other kid and this drama would have made great comedy to share at parties, but it would have been like making fun of a molested child or a guy paralyzed during a carjacking. Just twisted.

"It's not like your gonna disappear off the face of the earth. I promised, and we will, just as soon as we get back." Marvin nodded to Danny. "Isn't that right?"

"Absolutely." Not totally sure of what he had agreed to do, but the slight smile on Andy's face was worth it. A whole bunch better than tears.

Marvin said, "Let's do this. The weekend after Danny and I get back from Europe we will drive to Baltimore to see you."

Andy stared at his feet, nudging a dried glob of gum on the platform. "You better call first 'cause I may not be there anymore."

"What do you mean—you may not be there anymore?"

"If I don't like it at her house I'm not staying there. I'll stay with Jason until you and Danny get back."

"What makes you think you may not like it?"

Danny added, "You haven't been there yet and she could be tons of fun. You never know."

"You don't know my aunt."

"Neither do you," Marvin pointed out. "You haven't seen her since you were little."

"My dad said she was a pain in the butt. He couldn't stand her and she was his sister, so he should know."

Marvin sighed. "That was years ago. People change, Andy."

"So what? If my dad didn't like her I won't like her either. I'm just like my dad and I'm sure he had good reasons. I don't know why I couldn't just stay with Jason until you and Danny come back, my aunt can't do nothing. I'm almost eighteen."

"When we come back from Europe we'll take it from there, although I'm certain if you just give it a chance, you'll like it in Baltimore. If not, I'll talk with her. Is that fair enough?"

"I don't want to stay there and I don't care if she is nice to me. I'll come back to stay with you guys. You should just pick me up in Baltimore on your way home." He scowled. "You're happy to get rid of me. Why can't you just admit it?"

"Andy, you know that's not true."

"Totally not true," Danny said, wishing that didn't make him angry, but it did. After everything they'd done for the kid and after all his worrying about him since that night in the rain at the cemetery, he couldn't believe Andy would accuse them of trying to get rid of him. "I looked it up. There was no way to get you out of the country without a passport."

Marvin said, "You know I wanted to take you with us and I would have, had that been at all possible. You think it's easy for me to put you on a train today? You know, you're not making this any easier on Danny and me either."

"Sorry." Andy rubbed the side of his face with his sleeve.

The train rolled into the station, brakes squealing. The doors opened and people rushed out. A hole opened in Danny's gut and a lump lodged in his throat. He absolutely hated goodbyes. With a hard swallow, he grinned and smacked Andy on the back. "It sucks now, but when we get back, I'll drive up there and get you. To hell with your aunt."

Andy spit out a quick, shaky laugh.

"Legal, Danny. We have to do everything by the book," said Marvin.

He nudged Andy, "Dad's got friends at social services. If your aunt doesn't put up a stink, it'll be a snap."

A conductor stared impatiently at them. As they followed him to the door, Danny remembered how the kid in cowboy boots and his buddy with the skateboard had beaten the heck out of Andy, how they'd played him and nearly put the guy in the hospital or jail.

His chest tightened as Andy got on all alone. Who would he meet on the train? Would he make it all the way to Baltimore, stick by their plan? Or would he hop out somewhere along the way and disappear. What if he ended up lost again?

Andy turned back before the doors closed, smiling, eyes shiny with tears. "Bring me back a beer from Germany!"

Danny laughed. "You can have one when you go with us next time."

"Take care, Andy," Marvin hollered.

The doors closed and they followed Andy's progress through the train as he moved back to his seat. All they needed, Danny thought, was a bunch of steam and a blonde lady waving a red scarf. A real Hollywood moment. It didn't feel like the movies though. It felt like every film ever made had tried to put on the big screen what he felt right then and had totally bombed.

Andy took his seat toward the center of the passenger car. He waved and they waved back. Danny added a big smile trying to ignore how tormented the guy looked. They walked a few steps until the train moved too fast to keep up. Andy's face flashed once behind the glass, then disappeared.

Danny could barely talk on the way home. When they parked in the garage, he asked, "You think he's really gonna be okay? With his aunt Lily?"

His father frowned and said, "I hope so."

Not very encouraging, he thought and got out of the car.

Inside, the house already felt empty. Most of the stuff they kept out had been tucked away in preparation for leaving on their trip the next day.

The silence was shattered by the phone ringing and his heart leapt in surprise. He answered, "Hello?"

"Hey," Ryan said. "I'm running late, but I should be there before dinner."

"That's cool," Danny said, shocked he'd forgotten that a half dozen friends were gonna stop by and say adios.

"Andy get off okay?"

No, not really he thought. "Yeah. He's on his way to Baltimore."

"Cool."

For the rest of the night, Danny hung out, ate pizza, and laughed with the guys. Once in a while, someone would say something about Andy or mention something that made Danny think of him and he'd have to force himself not to get all emo'd out about the whole thing. The excitement of going to Germany helped put the worst out of his mind though.

The phone rang around nine. The caller ID showed Andy's aunt's number and Danny went into the bedroom where it was quiet. He answered a real grin on his face for the first time that night. "Hey, how was the trip?"

"Long and bor-ring! I got here around eight-thirty. Her ankle biter won't stop barking. Are you done packing?"

Danny could hear the dog in the background and it already drove him crazy. "Yes, all done."

"Is your dad there? I want to talk to him real quick 'cause I can't stay on the phone long. She fixed supper and wants me to eat before it gets cold."

His father took the phone. Dying to hear what was being said, Danny watched him, listening.

"I won't forget... I know...three weeks... Right... Okay... Do you want to talk to Danny again? ...you take care."

Marvin handed him the phone.

"It's me again."

"I can't wait for you to get back. There are like no kids my age in the apartments here. Only old people. Anyway, have a great time in Europe. I got to get off the phone. She's asking me to come eat now. Bye."

The phone went dead. Danny exhaled and slumped happily in his chair. Andy sounded all right, like maybe he was gonna be okay after all. He shouldn't have worried.

When everyone left and the house fell silent again, Danny climbed the stairs slowly to his room. He stopped by the computer room Andy had used. His dad stood in the middle of the floor, sliding the white, number twenty-four jersey onto a hanger. "Guess he forgot this one."

Danny didn't know what to say. "We'll keep it for him."

His father nodded. "You headed to bed?"

"Yeah," he said.

They said goodnight and Danny went to his room, closing the door behind him. He lay that night in bed, listening to how silent everything was. Even the crickets seemed silent, like they knew bad weather was on the way and had fled for safer territory. The thought didn't comfort him.

The rush to the airport to give them plenty of time to get

through security and find their gate kept Danny too occupied to think about Andy. Even if he had the time though, he felt so much better about it all today. Germany rocked and Andy would be fine with his aunt. He even felt sort of goofy for being all worried about it to begin with.

The Frankfurt airport was an amazing place, full of proud German construction. The amount of glass covering the structure made the whole place feel airy and bright. A bakery teased them with the comforting aroma of fresh rolls and sweet pastries. In comparison to the airport back home, this one took the prize for cleanest and best arranged.

No sooner had they gotten their luggage and dragged it toward the exit, did they hear their names. "Marvin! Danny!"

His uncle Klaus strode to them with long lanky legs, huge slender hands opened as wide as his grin. He embraced them both briefly then took a bag each from Marvin and Danny. "How was your flight? Did you get a pretty attendant, Danny? One of those blue-eyed blondes with big—"

"It was a man," Marvin said, laughing. He asked Klaus how he and the family were doing in German.

Danny did okay, understanding more than he could speak himself, but for the most part, they were kind enough to use English around him—except when they wanted to tease him about his accent. Virginia had seeped into his German and even he admitted the mix could be comical.

Outside, the air was a dry seventies and fresh. He inhaled deeply, eager to move around after being on the plane so long.

Klaus led them to his VW that looked no different from

the day he brought it home. Danny remembered the mess in his backseat and was glad his uncle wouldn't be visiting them before he got a chance to clean it out.

"Ann and Tanja can hardly wait to see you, Danny," Klaus said.

Danny met his uncle's gaze in the rearview mirror. "Is Tanja still in love with that Zach kid?"

"He's popular here," Klaus said. "All the girls love him. Better, I think, to like one boy than to be crazy about all boys, no?"

Danny smiled. "Yeah, guess you're right."

"What about you? Girlfriend now?"

Danny shook his head. "There's a girl at work I like, but she's dating some dork from Burger King. Dad tell you about Andy?"

"No." Klaus glanced at Marvin. "Who is this Andy?"

As his father explained, Danny watched Frankfurt speed by. If ever he had a reason to want to live in Germany, it would have to be the autobahn. A car going a hundred and sixty was something you only saw on TV when they were being followed by an entire police force.

He only wished Andy was there to see it with them.

CHAPTER 21

A Bitter Day

Ten days into their visit, Danny got up early, not sure why. The house was quiet, even with the sun coming up and the birds making a racket. He padded through the house toward the kitchen and poured himself a glass from the pitcher of half juice and half carbonated water his Aunt Ann kept in there.

The houses on the street could have come from a postcard. White plaster and dark wood in geometric patterns made even the most diverse arrangement of landscaping seem uniform. That was how it was here, he thought—all neat and orderly. Maybe that's where his dad got the need to make sure everything was the way it should be, why he took in all those kids and tried to give them the sort of neat and orderly life that made him so happy, too.

"Morning."

Danny turned and saw his dad in the kitchen, already pulling out what he needed to prepare the morning coffee. "Hey, Dad."

"You're up early." He filled the carafe. "Sleep okay?"

Danny nodded and took a gulp of his juice. "What's the time difference between here and Baltimore?"

"Six hours. Thinking of giving Andy a call?"

"Yeah, just to say hi. See how things are working out

for him, y'know?"

"I think it's a great idea. Let's not put it on their bill here though. I've got a card to use."

Danny waited, feeling nervous and not knowing why. Would Andy be like totally depressed? Nah, probably having a great time. Relatives mostly liked to treat you great at first, sort of like a honeymoon or something. After you spent too much time around each other, even the coolest of them could turn into real pains.

"Here you go." His father held the phone out.

Danny took it in time to hear the final ring before it was answered.

"Hello?" The aunt said.

"Hi, um," what did he call her? Mrs. Lily? "Is Andy there?"

"He ain't here," she said, her high-pitched voice like the squawking bird from Aladdin. "Never even slept in his bed. I think he took off. He wrote just the most nasty stuff about me. That kid's gonna give me a heart attack I tell you. A heart attack, you hear me?"

"Yes."

His father gave him a sharp look and raised his eyebrows.

"Maybe you should talk to my dad." Danny handed the phone back before either of them could object.

Frowning, he accepted the receiver. "Hello?"

The juice gurgled in his belly. More than ever he wished he'd tried harder to have Andy come with them. Maybe they could have made up a story about political asylum or something, considering what a tyrant Aunt Lily was.

"When did you last see him?"

Oh, that didn't sound good. The muscle in his father's jaw jumped and he stared at the floor.

"Are you sure he ran away? Maybe he went to a friend's and just didn't call."

That didn't sound like Andy, who apologized like crazy if he even *thought* he'd upset someone.

"What did the notes say?" He changed colors—first a nervous pale, then an angered red. "Did you call his friends? What about Jason? What do you mean you wouldn't let him see Jason?"

Danny shook his head, trying to warn his dad to calm down
before he blew a gasket.

"Well, did you call anyone? The police?"

His dad shook his head at him, as if to say he couldn't believe what he was hearing. "If he turns up, call me at this number immediately." He made sure she wrote it down. "Reverse the charges then. Call collect, whatever you have to do. Just let me know when he comes back or if you find him."

His father hung up. "That woman is a…a piece of work. Andy's run away and I can't say I blame him. She was more angry he'd inconvenienced her than scared for him. We should have found a way to bring him here."

"Where do you think he went?" Danny asked, imagining Andy wandering all over Baltimore and running into someone else wearing cowboy boots.

"I don't know. Somewhere familiar, I would bet. Most of them do. Maybe his house or ours. Even his friend Jason.

Do you have Jason's number?"

Danny shook his head. "I didn't think to pack it. It's on my desk back home."

"She's not even looking for him." Marvin stared at his son, the unasked question hanging in the air between them.

Danny didn't know what to say. He wanted to fly home right then and there and look for him, but they were in Germany and that was an awful lot to convince a father to do.

His dad sighed and scrubbed his unshaven jaw. "Damn. We gotta go back, don't we?"

"Yeah," Danny said, surprised. "I think the next four days would really suck for both of us if we just sat around here."

He nodded, the rubbing hand moving to the back of his neck. "All right. I'll wake up Klaus and Ann. Get your things together."

Part IV

Nothing Makes Sense Anymore

CHAPTER 22

Long Train Coming

After two hours, Andy wanted to get up and stretch his legs, but he wanted more not to be remembered as the geeky kid who couldn't sit still. Only another thirty minutes or so before they rolled into Newport News anyway. Farmlands and small towns flashed by under a low-hanging sky. Like my life, he thought, moving fast and gloomy.

Baltimore far behind him, he should be relaxed. Instead, his options all seemed bleak. Normal felt so far away, out of his grasp. Like something dreamed up for other people, something not meant for him.

He would be all right.

Snarling at his reflection, he turned away from the window. He was tired of telling himself everything would be all right because it never was. Just when he thought things were going along fine, *Bam*! Everything was destroyed. He didn't know how anyone could trust life, he only knew he didn't.

His dream about the cars, Marvin and Danny and all his friends—that would never happen. What would they say if they could hear his thoughts now? What would they think of that dream? He bet they'd understand, that they wouldn't think he was brainless or something. How he wished he could talk to them.

He pulled his notepad and pen from his backpack and wrote about everything until his hand began to cramp. When he did get to talk to them, he wanted to remember every detail, to make them understand why he'd broken his promise to stay with Aunt Lily and why Marvin shouldn't be angry with him.

It really mattered that they understand.

As they neared the station, the passengers around him gathered their belongings. He had nothing to gather. What would he find when he got into the station? Cops? FBI? Whole camera crews waiting to watch the capture of runaway Andy Riley and the end of a nationwide manhunt?

No one does that for runaways.

Maybe Aunt Lily had been right. Maybe he was too dumb and clumsy to take care of himself. But he didn't plan on taking care of himself, not really. He planned at staying at his old house. Probably no one had bought the place yet and that meant technically, it still belonged to him, right? He could stay there a few days, get Jason to bring him food from his house—stuff the Mitchells wouldn't miss.

Going back to his old neighborhood, being near his house, those were good things. Nothing he did could get his life back to the way it used to be, but at least he wouldn't have to deal with Aunt Lily. They stopped and he stood with the other passengers, walking in an all-too familiar shuffle toward another exit.

He'd been on trains, trucks, buses and an airplane in the last two months, traveled more in one summer than his whole life. The only home he really had in all that time was with Danny and his dad—and now he'd betrayed Marvin and let Danny down.

He was falling with no one to catch him.

Following everyone else, he headed for the doors. He stepped outside, taking a deep breath of hometown air. Another ride later, this time a city bus, he stood at the end of his neighborhood. Everything had seemed to have gotten so much bigger, greener than he remembered. Or he had shrunk, one of the two.

Their street was at the top of a gradual incline and he'd forgotten how unexpectedly tiring going uphill could be. When he got to his street, he stayed across, watching the front of the house. There was no sign on the lawn advertising it was for sale, which was good. Maybe if his Aunt Lily didn't remember to sell the house, he could have it when he turned eighteen in few months. Mom and Dad would like that, he thought, especially if he kept it the way they had left it behind.

The lush lawn had been mowed recently. A hot summer day many years ago his father had walked along behind him, showing him how to use the mower—like a normal father and son. How long ago that had been, an eternity it seemed. They were all supposed to grow old there. Where had all their things gone? The pictures, the box of stuff his mom had saved for him after his father's funeral, the things she had saved from when he was little. Where had it all gone? He had let all traces of his family vanish, lost forever.

Weeks ago, he and Jason rollerbladed on the sidewalk in front of the house, and when they got thirsty, they went inside together. Just like that, walked right in and asked if they could have soda. His mom stood in the hall that day, asking if he was hungry and if Jason wanted to stay for dinner.

No one was in there anymore.

Could he stand to go in alone? Sneak in through a basement window and make himself a place to sleep? He started to step off the curb when a blue four-door sedan slowed down and parked directly in front of his house. His heart pounded.

It doesn't mean anything.

A man sat behind the wheel, gathering his belongings before exiting the car.

Probably just the real estate guy.

The front door, *his* old front door, opened and a woman leaned against the frame, arms crossed in a way that reminded him of his mom. She smiled at the man who exited from the car and strode up the walkway. Two small girls ran out of the house.

"Daddy!"

"Daddy!"

They danced in front of him, their arms held out as he picked up both, hugged and kissed each on the cheek. "How are my girls?"

Andy couldn't breathe, couldn't blink, ready to shatter. The mom kissed the dad and they went inside and closed *his* door on *him.*

Shut out.

I can't take this anymore. Not anymore.

Danny tried to sleep on the plane home, but his gut was twisted in knots so bad, he couldn't get comfortable. He'd doze off, had that sense of falling, then jerked awake.

"Danny," his father said. "We can't do anything until we land. Get some sleep, okay?"

"I'm trying," he whispered. Other passengers slept around them, lights turned low in the cabin. "You think he ran into those kids again? The ones from the flea market?"

"No," he said. "He's hurt and upset, but he's not dumb. I doubt he'd go back to Virginia Beach again, especially alone."

Danny considered that for a moment. Andy had a way of wanting to please people all the time. "What if he's, like, I don't know, gotten in with worse guys?"

"Let's not borrow trouble." He patted Danny's shoulder. "Sleep, okay? You'll need the rest when we land."

"I'll try," he said, laying his head against the seat and staring at the stars out the window. Cool at first, six hours into the nine-hour flight—he would have preferred MTV or anything that would help keep his mind off Andy. He had known something bad would happen and he didn't listen to himself because he thought it was just useless worry about Andy again, a kid who had issues. But he'd known it was more and lied to himself.

By the time they hit Hampton, his nerves were stretched to the breaking point. The ride home took too long, every red light excruciatingly painful. "We have to find him, Dad. We have to."

At the house, they left their luggage in the doorway, not bothering to close the door behind them.

"I'll check for messages." Marvin picked up the phone and dialed to access voicemail. Danny waited, exhausted, but pulse pounding all the same. His dad punched a few more buttons, then shook his head.

He said, "Call his aunt, Dad, see if she's heard anything. Put it on speaker so I can hear too, okay?"

"Okay." He dialed the number and at first it rang and rang.

When he thought she wouldn't answer, she finally did. "Hello?"

"It's me, Marvin—and Danny's here too."

"Did you have a nice flight?" She asked.

What did that matter? Danny scowled.

"Yes, fine. Any word from Andy?"

"No."

His heart sank.

"Did you get a hold of Jason? Call anyone? Ask around; see if your neighbors saw him?"

"No. Remember, he said he didn't want me coming after him." She sounded defensive. "I suffer from poor health, you know, and I don't have tons of money to buy gas running after a kid who doesn't want to be found. Besides, I'm feeling sickly today because I can't find my pills anywhere. I think the dog might have hidden them from me. I wouldn't be any use to you even if I had them. They make me sleepy."

"Call my cell phone if you hear from him. We'll start looking now." Marvin hung up the phone. "Can you believe her?"

"No, and you'd get mad if I called her all the names I want to." Danny wanted to smash her face in. Who could be that cold? "I'll get Jason's number."

Andy's feet hurt. Tears dried on his face, slightly itchy as the salt tightened the skin. He had no more tears to cry. The cemetery fence rose up at the end of the street. If anyone cared about him now and God wanted him to live, someone would find him before it was too late. He stepped onto the gravel path with a sigh of relief. He could rest soon and he had no regrets. Nothing would get better, only worse. He counted each crunching step to his parent's graves.

One…two…three…four…

Danny dashed into the kitchen. "I found Jason's number."

"Thank God." His dad took the paper and dialed quickly.

"Speaker, Dad." Danny hovered at his elbow.

He pressed the button as a man answered. "Hello?"

"Hello, yes, my name is Marvin and I'm a friend of Andy Riley? Is this Mr. Mitchell?"

"Yes… Can I help you?"

Danny wanted to scream at the man, to say *Yes! Look for him! Find him!*

"Andy's disappeared from his aunt's house in Baltimore and we thought maybe he was with you?"

"No," he said, dashing Danny's last hope. "Haven't seen the poor kid since we put him on the plane. They sold his old house, y'know, wasn't on the market but like a week. Heard it was a quick sale. They got a good deal. I don't think he'd come back here."

"What about Jason? Maybe he's seen him?"

Danny held his breath and stared at his father as they

listened to the off-phone conversation happening between father and son. He sunk even further when he overheard Jason's reply.

Mr. Mitchell came back. "No, he hasn't seen him either."

"Thanks," Marvin said, and gave him both the house and cell phone numbers in case he saw Andy.

Danny frowned, trying hard to think of anything Andy might have mentioned, anywhere else he had even gone while he stayed with them. "Where do you think he is?"

"If he's not here, and he's not at his old house—"

Danny nodded, coming alive as his hope renewed. "Then he's at the same place he went when he ran away from here."

"The cemetery."

They both ran for the garage.

Seventy-seven...seventy-eight...   seventy-nine...
"Eighty."

Andy stood in front of the graves, set his backpack down and sat. He imagined his parents were both relieved to see him again and happy to have someone tend their graves. They couldn't fend for themselves, after all and relied on him.

Crazy talk...

"Sorry I didn't come sooner," he whispered, tearing out a handful of weeds that had sprouted by his father's headstone. No, he wasn't going crazy. He knew his parents and they wouldn't want to be remembered by an untidy grave.

He smoothed his hair, messy after all the walking and sweating to get there. His mom liked it best when he made an effort to keep it neat. He pulled the folded photograph of his father out of his rear pocket, straightened it gently, and placed the photo neatly in front of the headstone.

"Sorry I don't got a picture of you, Mom." He sighed. "Dad, you were right about Aunt Lily all along." He put a hand on the thick grass above his father's remains. "I know you would have done anything in your power to keep me from having to live with her if you could."

He swallowed and his hands no longer shook. "She was so mean to me and I don't blame you for ignoring her all these years. You knew how she was."

Gently, calmly, he placed a hand over his mother. "Mom, please forgive me. I've done wrong. I got mad and...and...jealous. I can't undo what I've done. All this is my fault."

He started to cry. *Why couldn't he hear them, just a little?*

A small, white butterfly floated in the air, making lazy circles. A sign from his mother, he thought. Andy smiled and wiped the tears dripping from his chin. He didn't want to be anywhere else in the world. Nowhere else in the world for him to go. He couldn't leave them now. Not ever.

"Sorry I wasn't strong enough, Mom."

He freed the pills from the sock at the bottom of the bag. A half-empty bottle of water rolled out. It came to rest against his mother's headstone, almost as if she had stopped it from going too far away, to make sure he had something to drink to wash the pills down, like when he was little and sick. He smiled and reached for the bottle.

Thanks, Mom.

He unscrewed the top on the pill bottle and poured the small, white capsules into his palm. They filled the shallow well of his upturned hand. One final ticket, one final trip, one final ride—to be with his parents forever. He opened the water bottle to wash down the pills. He took them, a few at a time, swallowing until they were all gone.

He lay down between the graves, stared at the sky and waited. Nothing happened.

He read the empty plastic container *Prescription sleeping aid take one by mouth at nighttime.* Just one? Andy grinned, starting to feel a little floaty. "Oops."

He tossed the container aside. Not a soul to save him now.

No soles of no souls coming for no soul.

He knew he didn't make sense and he didn't care. Minutes passed, maybe half an hour. His lids grew weighty, his vision distorted, his mind wandered.

Mom, some new family moved into our house. I saw them today. They look nice.

Cold sweat slid down the sides of his forehead, pooling in the hair at his temples. "I'm tired."

He let himself drift, watching an airplane wander soundless overhead.

I was in one, Dad. Did you know?

Light, comfortable, he followed the white vapor trail drawn peacefully across the blue. He closed his eyes, overcome and taken by an upward draft, his own weight absent. Surrounded by a pure white glare, only the sound of traffic nearby let him know he was still on earth, still there…

CHAPTER 23

Plunged into Purgatory

Danny longed for the speed of the Porsche as his dad drove the station wagon. They crawled through afternoon rush hour traffic. Forced to use the wagon because the Porsche was almost out of gas, he urged his dad to drive aggressively, pointing to lanes that showed promise of moving even a smidgen faster, ignoring hostile stares, and honking alike.

He said, "We're never gonna find him. He could be anywhere in the world."

"I don't think so."

"Maybe he's with a friend in Baltimore. We should wait at the house. He could show up later or call his aunt." Danny didn't want to believe Andy could really be at the cemetery because the meaning in that scared him to his toes.

"She said he didn't make any friends. No. He'd come here. This is all he knows."

Danny prayed that if they did find him there, he was safe and sound.

Marvin's phone rang and he handed it to his son.

Danny answered.

"Hey, this is Jason," the kid said. "Did you find Andy yet?"

"No. You find out anything else?"

"I asked the lady who moved into his house. She said she's been home all day and didn't see anyone."

"Okay. We think we may know where to find him."

"Where?"

Danny swallowed. "At the cemetery."

"That's…not good. Call me back if you find him, okay?"

"We will."

He disconnected the call and turned all his attention to wishing away the traffic jam. The sun was nearly gone by the time they got to the cemetery and parked. They jogged to the Riley's plot. A few feet in, Danny spotted Andy lying on the grass between his parents' graves. His heart drummed in his ears.

"Andy," Danny called, but he didn't respond. A half yard away, an empty pill bottle glowed a dull orange in the grass. "*I think the dog hid them,*" she had said. "Oh, no…"

His father knelt, put an arm behind Andy's shoulders, and lifted him up, shouting in his ear, "Andy wake up! C'mon, wake up! Don't do this now."

He didn't even blink.

"Dad?" Danny sounded scared, small. "Is he breathing?"

He nodded and put his ear to Andy's chest. "It's faint, but there. Stay with him, I'll get the car."

"Please, Andy," Danny begged. Andy's clothes were soaked and he felt much heavier than expected. "Wake up now, okay? We're back! We came back from Europe. You can stay with us. Wake up, please!"

Danny's throat closed. They had to get him to the hospital. The skin around his lips tinged blue, his eyelids pale, the faint spread of veins above the lashes seemed darker somehow.

Please God, don't let Andy die... Please...

Headlights illuminated his pale, gray face as Marvin drove the wagon right up to the grave. He hopped out, tossed Andy's bag and the medicine container in the car, then helped Danny drag Andy into the backseat. He got in beside him as his dad drove. What could he do? "Andy, wake up, wake up buddy, c'mon, please?"

Marvin sped through the dwindling traffic, using the high beams and horn to get around drivers and slip through intersections before flooring it again. Danny held Andy upright as best he could. His head against Danny's shoulder, he held a hand to his mouth and felt his fading breath. Much, much too long between inhale and exhale he thought.

"Is he breathing?" Marvin hollered, whipping around a corner.

"Barely," Danny shouted back, trying to brace them from careening around the back seat. Andy's hands grew icy. He whispered in his ear, pleading, nose and eyes burning with tears. "Stay with me. Please stay here, Andy. Please."

He prayed that somewhere deep down he could convince him to fight, to stay here and live with them. "Just hold on. Hold on. We won't leave you. I won't leave you. You're like my brother, okay? Almost there."

He counted the seconds between respirations, desperately searching for any sign Andy wanted to wake up. Five seconds, then seven, and finally ten between each breath. The increase alarmingly fast.

Make it to the hospital.

Please, make it to the hospital.
Make it just that far.

"I'm almost there," Marvin called. "Hang on, Andy."

He didn't listen. As Marvin screeched to a halt at the emergency doors, Andy released a series of short, fast breaths.

Oh God, no…

"Andy?" Danny held him tighter, hardly able to talk. "Andy? Andy!"

He released one great exhale. His hand squeezed Danny's faintly and he went utterly still. A tear rolled from his eye.

"Andy?" Danny choked back a sob. "No, oh no…"

Not like this.

"Come back, Andy," he wept. "Please come back."

"Danny?" Marvin stood at the open back door, leaning into the backseat. "Is he…?"

His throat closed and unable to answer, he shook his head. A man and woman in hospital green ran out the doors. The man turned back to the woman as soon as he got a look inside. "Get a gurney!"

Then his dad and the man tried to pull Danny away. He didn't want to go; he didn't want to leave Andy. He promised he wouldn't leave him and if he broke that promise Andy would slip away for good.

"It's okay, I've got him," the man said gently as the woman reappeared with the gurney.

They transferred him from the car to the bed and the woman asked, "What happened to him?"

What hadn't happened to him? We left him.

"Overdose." Marvin grimaced.

They rushed alongside them as they took Andy inside.

"I have the empty container. The pills he took." His dad went back outside.

"I've got no pulse," the man called as they pushed through a set of double doors.

A lady wearing glasses held her hands up in front of Danny. "Sorry, you can't go in there. You'll have to wait out here."

His father returned, breathing hard, eyes wild. He held up the bottle. "This is what he took."

She accepted the bottle. "Do you know how full it was?"

They both shook their heads.

"I'll make sure they get this. Please take a seat in the waiting room. We'll let you know what's happening as soon as we can."

They turned away in unison, plodding with exhaustion to the sterile and unpleasant waiting area. Numb, Danny sat down, elbows on his knees, head in his hands and stared at the tile between his wet sneakers. Andy had to be okay. They could revive him, right? Bring him back?

Please bring him back.

His father's hand rubbed his shoulders and he wanted to lay his head down and cry. "I never saw anyone like that before. You think... you think he's gonna be okay?"

"I hope so." His voice was thick.

Oh, Dad, don't you cry, Danny thought, if you start crying I'm gonna lose it.

He stood, too nervous to stay seated and began to pace,

walking to the doors and looking through the slim windows, then returning to his dad. Back and forth he went, over and over again. He finally sat again, not knowing what do.

"We shouldn't have gone to Frankfurt." Danny sniffed, rubbing his nose with the cuff of his shirt. "This would have never happened."

His father put an arm around his shoulders and said, "You can't blame yourself."

But I will, and I will, and I will...

"Sir?"

They both looked up.

His dad asked, "Is there word?"

The lady shook her head. "I need some information from you."

He answered her questions, each one making this whole thing all the more real for him. *What's his home address? How are you related? Medical history? Has he been suicidal before?*

Danny barely noticed when his father and the nurse led them to a more private room. Alone together in the room, his father's tears weakened the last of Danny's strength to hold it together. He wept.

By far, it was the longest wait he ever had, an eternity of not knowing, of being torn up inside. Both leapt to their feet when a doctor came into the room.

"How's he doing?" his father asked.

Danny asked, "Is he okay?"

The redheaded doctor raised a brow at them. "Let's sit down so I can go over a few things with you."

His dad said, "I don't want to sit down. I want to know

how Andy is doing. Is he okay?"

"They were still working on him. I know his heart had stopped when you brought him in." They must have looked horrified because he paused and said, "Would you like me to check again?"

They nodded. He left, then returned within minutes. "Is he your son, or a family member?"

"Andy's my nephew," his dad lied.

"I'm sorry. There's never any easy way to say this. They did all they could. He didn't make it."

An anguished cry rose in his chest and Danny did his best to hold it back. He fell back into the chair, bent at the waist, and laced his fingers on the back of his head.

No. No. No. No.

He couldn't think; he just rocked as his father held him. The doctor and his dad continued to speak but he could barely hear them.

Andy is dead. Andy. Andy. He's dead. Oh my God, he's dead. He's dead.

"He took a massive amount of the medication. We can't say how many for sure, but we believe the prescription had recently been filled. I'm sorry for your loss."

"Can we see him?" His father gasped, voice gruff and wobbly.

"I'll have them prepare Andy for your visit."

Prepare? Visit?

Danny wanted to punch the doctor. Prepare? Who was he to prepare anything? He didn't know Andy. He didn't know him. Andy didn't want to be prepared for a *visit*. How sick was that? The doctor left before Danny could yell at him. Instead, he turned to his father. "He's gone, Dad. How can Andy be gone? How can he be dead?"

Marvin's shoulders shook from the power of his own grief. "I don't know."

The room grew colder and colder as Danny emptied the tissue box on the table. He swallowed hard, leaned back, and turned burning eyes to the ceiling. "Oh man, I don't know if I can take this. I can't believe it."

"You'll be all right, Danny. It hurts like hell now, and it won't go away soon, but you will be okay."

Beneath his father's measured words, Danny heard the fear…the fear he might want to join Andy to escape this pain. He could never put his father or anyone through this sort of grief. Never. He wiped at his wet face again as the door opened and the doctor returned.

"Follow me." He led them through corridor after corridor.

Danny did manage to keep up, but it was hard to see through the tears. He had never felt so much pain in his whole life. Not even when his mom got remarried and moved away. Not even when Ryan had moved out. Nothing compared to this explosive sadness.

The doctor opened a door for them. "He's in here. Take as much time as you need."

Andy lay beneath a white sheet, his face turned to the bright lights above the gurney. His dark hair waved away from his temples, pooling slightly against the mattress. Longer somehow than Danny had realized. He needed a haircut.

No. No haircuts for him. Never again.

259

His dad went around to the other side, passing beyond Andy's slack, peaceful face.

Oh man, Andy, why? You could have been with us. Why?

His father placed a hand on top of Andy's hair, tears streaming down his face. He whispered, "I'm so sorry."

Danny put his hand over his father's, the tips of his fingers touching Andy's scalp—already cold. He uttered low, through his clogged throat, "I'm sorry, too."

His dad reached across Andy's chest for Danny's other hand and he grasped it, holding hard like a man falling off a cliff. They stood that way for a moment, all three connected in a way he couldn't have imagined in his worst nightmares. He wept openly.

Guilt, sorrow, so much careened through his head. Mere minutes had passed since the doctors tried to save his life, thirty, maybe forty minutes. Head down, Danny wondered that he and his dad were the only ones there. To the doctors at the hospital, Andy was just some kid who OD'd, something they had probably seen a thousand times. He wasn't the kid who thought bowling was the best thing in the world, who only wanted a ride in the Porsche, or who loved his mom so much he wanted to keep the rain off her grave.

The doctors all got to go home to their families. Danny couldn't take Andy home. He would have to leave him, here, under a generic sheet in a hospital by himself.

"I can't go, Dad." He squeezed his father's hand tighter. "I can't just leave him here."

He didn't say anything, but they stayed with Andy for a full half hour. They came home too late from a trip he would forever regret. His legs didn't want to carry him, but somehow, he walked out of that room, an unrelenting deep ache inside him.

What did you do to us, Andy? Why?

Danny heard Andy in his head, the familiar words a spear of guilt within him.

Don't leave me. Don't go. I don't want to be alone. Stay with me. Please.

He stopped at the door, broken by that imagined and unbearable plea. It drove him insane, shredded his heart.

He couldn't sleep. Danny sat at the kitchen table, a cold cup of hot chocolate his dad made hours earlier in front of him. Near three in the morning, his eyes burned, red and raw from all the crying. Beyond tired, he wished he could close his eyes without seeing Andy's corpse under those lights. His father snored softly on the couch, sounding stuffy from the crying he had done.

Andy's backpack was slung over the chair across from him. After calling Jason and Andy's aunt, they didn't have the stamina or strength to touch his belongings, to feel them in their hands.

Right now, that was all he wanted to do. He slid the cup aside and pulled the backpack to him. The smell of rain, the fabric damp, worried him that the belongings might be ruined and wet. The zipper sounded loud in the quiet house and he held his breath, not sure why. If his dad woke, he wouldn't mind if Danny looked through Andy's stuff. He didn't wake though and he opened the backpack the rest of the way.

Andy's wallet lay on top of the dirty clothes crammed in the bag. He flipped the brown leather fold-over open and was greeted by Andy's serious face on a school I.D. He closed it quickly, unable to face those eyes right then. A beaten spiral notebook peeked between a shirt and a pair of socks.

Danny stared, wondering if he meant to torture himself more, or if he just wanted to feel closer to Andy. He never figured out why Andy blamed himself for his mom's death.

He understood now.

The book was damp, but not wet and when he drew it out, he braced himself for what he might find. He opened the cover and flipped through the pages slowly. Poems, doodles, a few pages like a diary, he scanned them all with weary eyes. He froze at the end, catching his and his father's names neatly written across the top of the page.

Tell Marvin and Danny about this dream.

I woke up on a bus, somewhere in Virginia, horns honking next to my window and when I looked, it was Marvin and Danny, and all my best friends I had made living at Marvin's house. They were driving their crazy cars and Jason was with them. Danny was in the passenger seat of the Porsche holding up a large handwritten sign "Welcome Back Andy" I was so happy that I had people who cared and loved me so much that they got in their cars to meet up with the bus before I arrived at the station.

There was more, but he couldn't read it. He put his hands over his face and sobbed.

His father made all necessary funeral arrangements for Andy and once Aunt Lily understood he meant to pay for it, allowed them to bury him where he chose to die, between his parents. The day of the funeral, Danny sat in front of the coffin unmoving. If there was any chance a soul lived on after the body died, he wanted Andy to know he was there. Deep down, he believed he did know, and maybe it made it a little easier on him, to know he would be missed—that people did care.

Lily came down from Baltimore and Andy's grandpa came to the funeral to pay their last respects. During the following procession to the cemetery, Danny arranged to have his friends drive their souped-up cars behind the hearse. His dad led them in the Porsche, Danny sitting beside him, holding up a hand-written sign that read "Welcome Back Andy." It was the closest he could come to honoring Andy's last requests and he knew he watched from up above, thrilled to see his dream come true.

As he stood beside the casket, before both his parents, he asked their forgiveness that while alive, he had failed Andy as a friend. That he was with his parents now, his family reunited, was his only consolation. He promised to spend as much time as he needed to visit him. And he did.

Every free minute he had, he spent at Andy's grave. Before his shift at the Food Lion, after he and Ryan went bowling, sometimes just when he wanted to go for a drive.

Nearly a year it took, before he found peace and felt a release, a sense that wherever his friend was now, he truly was okay.

CHAPTER 24

Being Strong and Moving On

Over the course of that first year, the mystery of those four days Andy couldn't or didn't want to remember bothered Danny. Between the time he landed in Newport News and when they first met him four days later at the flea market, something had happened to him.

He had said once, *"I totally murderized those memories. They don't exist. I go to the airport alone and I left alone. That's it. Besides, if I don't remember, it must not have been important."*

The possibility that something happened then to make him want to kill himself wouldn't leave Danny alone. His dad bugged him to tell him what was going on and because he didn't want to scare him, maybe give the impression he'd ever take his own life, he told him. Surprised he didn't think his son was a total lunatic, but actually had the same thoughts; Danny was relieved to have his help.

When his dad went to the airport, armed with a recent photograph of Andy to ask around, Danny called Jason. He asked him to find out what he could. When he called back, he said two neighbors remembered seeing him run out of his house that afternoon, but no one saw him come home from the airport.

His father came home hours later. "I asked cab drivers

and a bunch of the people who worked at the airport. No one remembered him."

"This is dumb," Danny said, frustrated. "What does it matter anyway?"

"It's a good idea," his dad offered. "I'd like some answers, too. Maybe it helps."

"Helps?"

"I feel responsible too, Danny. I should have seen the signs. I've worked with boys like him before. Don't know how I missed seeing it."

"It wasn't your fault, Dad," he said.

"Logically I know that, and you know that, but it doesn't make it any better, does it?"

Danny shook his head. "So what do we do?"

His dad sighed, rubbed the back of his neck, then brightened. "We could put an ad in the papers, in Newport News and in Virginia Beach."

"You think that will work?"

"Doubt it," he said. "But I'd rather try than always wonder."

"Yeah," Danny said. "Me too."

"I'll offer a small reward. That should help."

Over the next few weeks, a few people called who thought they may have seen him. Some were only after the reward money and their description of him was totally off the mark. All leads were dead ends.

Danny answered the phone on a late Sunday morning. An elderly lady from Norfolk called about a teenager who smashed car windows and tore up mailboxes in her neighborhood. She described a boy with dark hair, but a guy in the background, apparently her husband, said the kid was blond and that it happened a month after Andy died. She apologized and wished him luck.

When his dad renewed the ad for the last time, Danny had given up ever knowing what happened. Then a guy from Newport News called and said his younger sister talked about a kid she'd given his jersey to. This was one of the filters they'd agreed on. Not getting his hopes up, Danny asked, "What number was on jersey?"

"Twenty-four."

He sat up straight. "Can I talk to your sister?"

"She should be home in two days. She went to some concert in New York."

"Will you tell her to call?"

"I'll do that." He paused. "You think this is the kid you're looking for?"

"Yeah," Danny said, but ended the call quickly before he had to explain why and what had happened to Andy.

Those two days crawled by, Danny afraid to miss the call stayed as close to home as work allowed. His dad helped, promising to answer it quickly if he wasn't home. On the evening of the second day, he could hardly stand it and thought of calling the brother back to find out if he remembered to give her the message. He sat, staring at the phone, wanting it to ring and when it did, he picked it up before for the first jangle ended. "Hello?"

"Hi. My name's Sarah, you don't know but my brother said you were looking for a kid, about sixteen named Andy?"

"Yes, exactly," Danny said, standing. His father came in

from the other room and he gave him a thumbs up. "What do you remember?"

"A real polite, quiet kid. We ran into him on our way to a concert in Virginia Beach. It was raining cats and dogs and he was soaking wet. We stopped and asked if he wanted a ride. He looked so lost, y'know? Like he'd just escaped kidnappers or something, at least that's what I thought at first."

Danny nodded, knowing that look. "Yeah."

"Anyway, we tried to help him dry off and I gave him Darryl's jersey then."

"White, red sleeves, right, with the number twenty-four?"

"Yeah," she said. "You still looking for him?"

Danny heaved a big breath. "You think we could meet up somewhere? Talk some? I have the jersey, if you want it back."

Silence on the line. "He's not okay, is he?"

"No."

"Yeah, we can talk." She sounded sad. "Around six tomorrow night? I have to work today."

"Sure." He had to work himself at that time, but he'd switch with someone. "Where?"

"I could come to your house. My brother's got your number." She added the last with a little chuckle.

"Perfect." Danny gave her directions and hung up.

"Was that the sister?" his dad asked.

"Yeah, she'll be here tomorrow night, around six."

"Then we'll know."

"Yeah," he said. If she knew anything, that was. Worse,

268

he hadn't told her Andy had killed himself. While he wanted to know what she knew, he didn't want to be the one to tell her about his death. He couldn't wait for her visit, and dreaded it at the same time.

CHAPTER 25

Sarah's Visit

Just after six p.m. on a cloudy evening at the end of December, Sarah's red four-door Mazda stopped in front of the house. Danny met her on the sidewalk. He guessed she was in her early twenty's, about five foot four, brown curly shoulder length hair and aquamarine eyes. She wore a red coat that made her cheeks all rosy looking. She shook his hand and he prayed it didn't feel sweaty to her.

His dad held the door open for her and they all sat down in the dining room. She shrugged out of her coat and glanced at the short stack of photos Marvin had taken of Andy when he stayed with them.

They sat awkwardly until she tucked her hair behind her ear and said, "This is a great house. Love the view out these windows."

"Thank you." His dad smiled.

Danny slid the photos to her. "This him?"

"That's him, yes I'm positive." She lifted the top one to study closer. "Was he a runaway? Missing?"

"Something like that," his father answered. "He was vacationing with friends when he got the news his mother had been killed in a car accident. His dad died a few years before, so he...I guess had a hard time. He said he didn't remember the four days between his return home and coming to live with us."

She nodded and set the photo down. "Are you his stepfather?"

"No." He smiled sadly. "I would've liked to have been though."

"Can I see him?"

This was the moment Danny feared most. He looked to his dad, whose hand shook noticeably as he accepted the photographs back from her. "Andy died six months ago. He took his own life."

Sarah's jaw dropped "Oh my God. What happened? I mean, to make him do that?"

Danny did his best to explain about how they went to Germany and Andy had to live with his aunt. He hurried through it all, skipping big chunks so it wouldn't be quite as bad reliving everything. "That's where he got the pills, and he took them."

"We found him at the cemetery, between his parent's graves," his father said.

Tears welled in her eyes. "I… can I have something to drink?"

Danny reached behind him to the tissue box they kept on the counter and slid it across the table.

His father stood, "Coffee sound good?"

"Yes, great. Thanks," she said, offering a watery smile.

His dad asked, "Cream and sugar?"

"Yes, both please," she said, "I can't believe he killed himself. He didn't seem like the kind of guy who would do that. This is all so awfully sad. I didn't realize…"

Marvin brought her cup of coffee and sat back down.

"What do you remember?"

"I really didn't know him all that long, but he had a way about him. You know what I mean. Like a stray kitten you can't leave behind?" At Danny's nod she continued, "As I mentioned on the phone, we were on our way to a concert in Virginia Beach. I wanted him to wait for us, but he didn't, I guess, didn't want to be a trouble to us. I looked for him afterward. Jilly said she thought she saw him at a bus stop with a kid in a leather coat. I talked to her this morning because I kept thinking about what she'd said when we were driving back."

The phone rang and Danny excused himself to answer. "Hello?"

"Hey, this is Darryl. My sister there?"

"Yeah," he said and took her the phone. "It's your brother."

She rolled her eyes and said, "What's up? … No, I'm fine…No. The poor kid killed himself…yeah…I'll tell you all about it when I get back…okay…see ya then." She hung up and handed it back. "Sorry. You know how big brother's can be—strangers in a strange house. He just wanted to make sure you guys weren't wacko or something."

"Sounds like a good big brother." Marvin smiled.

Danny winced. He hadn't been much of any kind of brother to Andy. Here Sarah couldn't be away for half an hour and her brother was already checking to see if she was okay. He'd been in Europe for ten days and hadn't bothered calling once.

"You know," she said. "I really thought he would be okay, that he would find his way home and be all right. If I

272

had known his mom just died, I would have skipped the concert and stayed with him, helped him if I could. He really was a nice kid."

"I know what you mean. Wait here." His father went up the stairs and Danny knew where he was going.

A sense of finality, of resolution crept over him. When his dad came down the stairs, the jersey swaying gently on a hanger, he had to turn away quickly and swallow hard.

His dad took it off the hanger and handed it to her. "Here, you should take this."

"I never thought I'd see this again." She held it up by the shoulders, then folded it neatly and set it on the table, one hand spread across the numbers. "Gosh, it seems strange to think the last person who wore this isn't with us anymore. Are you sure you don't want to keep it? I mean, it seems like you were much closer..."

Danny shook his head. "No. We have some of his other things."

"Thank you, for returning it to me."

"You're welcome." His dad pointed to the numbers. "It was funny to see him in that because twenty-four is my lucky number. I thought...well, I don't know, that it was sort of a sign, in a way, for me to give this kid a chance."

She smiled. "Maybe it was."

In the quiet that followed, his father cleared his throat and asked uncomfortably, "Do you want cash or a check?"

"For what?"

"The reward."

Danny said, "Our ad offered a reward for information about Andy."

She shook here head. "No, that's all right. The jersey is payment enough. From what you told me, you deserved to have the information I could give you."

Sarah stood and shrugged into her coat, holding her purse and the jersey in one hand. "I'm sorry to leave so soon, but I've got a ton of stuff to do. I haven't even unpacked from my trip yet."

"Thank you so much for coming," his father told her.

"Yeah," Danny said. "Really, thanks a lot."

They walked her out to her car. Sarah got in and put the key in the ignition then paused and rolled down the window. "I'm glad he had that time with you guys. I bet you made him happy."

Danny heaved a sigh and his father said, "We did what we could."

Did they really?

Tears glimmered in her eyes and she started the engine. They watched her disappear down the street before starting back inside.

Had they really done what they could?

A snowflake landed on Danny's face, melting against the warmth of his skin. He looked up. More snow drifted down from the heavy white sky, like an answer from above.

He climbed the few steps to the door and thought that maybe yeah, maybe they had.

EPILOGUE

Remembrance and Anticipation

Danny headed off for college that following year. He could still picture Andy when he closed his eyes. How he looked when they first met, laughing in the Porsche, bowling at the alley with Ryan, and the day he got on the train north. Those were the memories he kept with him as time rushed on.

Andy once read aloud from some magazine. "*Happiness is a disease happy people suffer, I suffer my own diseases, but happiness isn't one of them.*"

Danny had laughed then, but now he sometimes wondered if anything could have stopped Andy. One of the courses he chose was psychology, looking up everything about suicide right away, trying to gain a deeper understanding. What he gained was a sense of acceptance and relief that he had been part of making Andy happy at least for a short while.

He kept a photo of Andy in his wallet and used his backpack, sort of like bringing Andy with him to college. A silly gesture, he knew, but he still used it, though the notebook was back at his dad's house, on a shelf in the computer room where the rest of what Andy had once cared about was stored.

Back in July, Danny and his dad drove to Virginia

Beach in the Porsche again. They went to the flea market and he found himself searching for Andy's face in the crowd. The trip was nothing like it had been before. The freedom, the light-hearted chatter, and smell of the ocean held no appeal. Silently, they drove back home. Danny never went back.

He sometimes wondered if he would ever see Andy again, in the afterlife, maybe. In English lit he read a poem as part of an assignment and whenever he thought of his lost friend, those words came to mind:

All is Well

By Henry Scott Holland

Death is nothing at all,
I have only slipped into the next room
I am I and you are you
Whatever we were to each other, that we are still.
Call me by my old familiar name,
Speak to me in the easy way which you always used
Put no difference in your tone,
Wear no forced air of solemnity or sorrow
Laugh as we always laughed at the little jokes we
enjoyed together.
Play, smile, think of me, pray for me.
Let my name be ever the household world that it
always was,
Let it be spoken without effect, without the trace of
shadow on it.
Life means all that it ever meant.
It is the same as it ever was, there is unbroken
continuity.

Why should I be out of mind because I am out of sight?
I am waiting for you, for an interval, somewhere very near,
Just around the corner.
All is well.

The End

278

If you've had thoughts of taking your own life, you aren't alone. Suicide is the third leading cause of death in teens. People do care and are waiting to help. Friends and loved ones are sometimes more difficult to approach when the pain is overwhelming. Comfort and guidance can be found in trusted, knowledgeable caregivers and professionals. The world is not better off without your unique and special qualities; there is help. If you or someone you know has expressed the desire to take their own life, please make use of the contacts offered below:

National Suicide Hotlines USA
United States of America
Toll-Free / 24 hours a day / 7 days a week
1-800-SUICIDE
1-800-784-2433
1-800-273-TALK
1-800-273-8255

Suicide…read this first.
http://www.metanoia.org/suicide/

Suicide Prevention, Awareness, and Support.
http://www.suicide.org/

A Matter of Life and Death…
http://suicide.com/

Martin Bartloff

Born in Werl, a small town in the North Rhine-Westphalia province of Germany, Martin was the youngest of five boys. As a child he strived to better himself and entertain others. Anything that had wheels fascinated him and he organized and performed daredevil bicycle events in his neighborhood.

Martin earned two European trade school diplomas before vacationing in the United States in August of 1991, a vacation he never returned from. He settled on the Virginia coastline where his fascination with all things vehicular led him to open his own European automotive business in 1994. To satisfy his need to entertain, Martin began his career as an author in 2007. Today he lives with his teenage son, in Hampton, Virginia.

CPSIA information can be obtained
at www.ICGtesting.com
Printed in the USA
BVHW040819110620
581031BV00004B/78